"Jake Randolph h

didn't introduce herself, he continued. "I'm a carpenter and want to offer my services." He looked toward the missing corner of the house. "Looks like you could use some help. My prices are the most reasonable you'll find around here."

Before Bruce, Brook might have been swayed by that approach, and "reasonably priced" certainly appealed to her. The man seemed pleasant enough, and looked okay as far as she could make out in the dusk, but she'd learned the hard way that appearances could be deceiving. "I'm in a hurry," she said truthfully. "I'll be glad to take your card."

His grimace matched his words. "Sorry. I didn't bring one with me."

It suddenly dawned on her that she'd warned Ben about talking to strangers. She wasn't setting a very good example. "Well, thanks anyway," she said, opening her car door wider. "I plan to get estimates from local carpenters."

She jumped in and slammed her door before he could say anything more and quickly started the engine. Looking in the rearview mirror as she drove away, she saw the man looking after her. Then he moved back from his window, started his truck, and drove away in the opposite direction.

Frankly, it seemed strange that the most reasonably priced carpenter in the area just happened along as she was moving in. But he did give her his name—if it was his real one. Oh, well, if he meant any harm, her broken windows and flimsy lock were an invitation.

YVONNE LEHMAN, an award-winning novelist, lives in the heart of North Carolina's Smoky Mountains with her husband. They are the parents of four grown children. In addition to being an inspirational romance writer, she is also the founder of the Blue Ridge Christian Writers' Conference.

Books by Yvonne Lehman

HEARTSONG PRESENTS
HP37—Drums of Shelomoh
HP82—Southern Gentleman
HP126—Mountain Man
HP201—A Whole New World
HP218—Hawaiian Heartbeat
HP290—After the Storm
HP305—Call of the Mountain

Somewhere
a Rainbow

Yvonne Lehman

Heartsong Presents

To Lori Marett, for her invaluable advice, and to Lynda Hopkins, ministry assistant, First Baptist Church, Hilton Head Island, SC, for her helpful information about the church on which I based many activities in this book (particularly the Sunrise Service).

You are cordially invited to attend the church when in the area of Hilton Head Island.

A note from the author:
I love to hear from my readers! You may correspond with me by writing: **Yvonne Lehman**
Author Relations
PO Box 719
Uhrichsville, OH 44683

ISBN 1-57748-618-8

SOMEWHERE A RAINBOW

All of the characters and events in this book are fictitious. Any resemblance to actual persons, living or dead, or to actual events is purely coincidental.

Cover illustration by Jocelyne Bouchard.

PRINTED IN THE U.S.A.

one

Brooke Haddon, driving in her compact car along Highway 278 toward the resort island of Hilton Head, recognized the depression settling over her like the gray sky over the ocean now that the sun had set. She tried to concentrate on five-year-old Ben's enthusiasm, to be as excited as her son. But all that he found so fascinating mimicked her own feelings of seven years ago. She'd been twenty then, with a model's face and figure, and as innocent and trusting as a child. Now she felt ancient—not so much in years as in experience.

She'd spent her honeymoon in blissful naiveté on this island off the coast of North Carolina. After a little more than three months of wedded bliss, her figure began to balloon out with pregnancy and then the marriage began to go downhill. Politician Bruce Haddon seemingly had everything going for him—except a happy marriage. Now Bruce was dead, Brooke was a single parent, and the only thing between her and homelessness, or dependence upon her parents, was the honeymoon cottage—a reminder of shattered hopes and dreams.

A year ago when she'd walked away from Bruce's funeral, she'd known his lover was being buried on the other side of town. She'd cried and grieved over an auto accident that took two young lives, a six-year failed marriage, a son without a father, for truth that would have to be told someday, and for all she'd lost—her livelihood and her self-esteem.

"Go slow, Mom," Ben pleaded, his dark eyes so like those of his late father's. "I want to see the alligators."

Brooke again went into her discussion of the alligators being in the lagoons and not along the main roads and the danger of getting close and then tried to divert his attention to the trees of the island, telling him about Spanish moss hanging from live oaks, pines, magnolias, palmettos, and palms. It didn't work!

"Anyway," she said resignedly, "we can't go alligator hunting tonight. I have to get to the realtor's office and pick up the key before dark."

Brooke had called from a rest station earlier to say she'd been delayed by road work. The realtor promised to meet her at the office, even though this was a Saturday evening. Brooke had wanted to come earlier in the week, but the realtor said the utilities wouldn't be hooked up before late Friday afternoon.

No unsightly signs cluttered the roadways to make the island look like a commercial playground. Slowing, Brooke peered through the trees, looking for the almost-hidden signs. With a sigh of relief, she saw a long structure with a sign reading "The Mall" on the front. She turned right and felt her stomach unknot as she saw a single car parked at the real estate office.

Ben was unbuckled and ready to hop out by the time Brooke stepped out and put her hand on the back-door handle. The poor child had been exceptionally patient on the two-day trip from Indiana. She'd stopped only to get food and a few hours sleep last night at a motel.

"Mrs. Haddon?" the realtor asked, as soon as Brooke and Ben popped through the door. She would be anxious to get out of there, Brooke was sure.

Brooke nodded. "I guess you're Jessica Lawler?" They'd talked several times on the phone. Jessica, a middle-aged woman dressed casually in slacks and a cotton blouse, gave

Brooke the impression she'd made a special trip to meet her at the office. "Sorry I'm so late," Brooke apologized, brushing back a strand of blond hair that had escaped her ponytail.

"It's okay," the realtor assured her, giving a gentle push to eyeglasses that covered friendly blue eyes set in a pleasant face. "Gave me an opportunity to catch up on some picky things I always put off and rarely get—" Her words stopped in mid-sentence as she saw Ben's adorable, smiling face and his outstretched hand. She leaned over and shook his hand.

"My name's Ben," he said, his big brown eyes, fringed with dark lashes the color of his curly black hair, charming her. By the time he was two years old, little Ben had been mimicking his father this way, realizing that it attracted and pleased other people. Brooke was all too aware that she had a big job ahead, instilling in Ben the kind of inner qualities that had been neglected while his father was alive.

"Would you like to have a seat?" Jessica asked, gesturing toward the chairs.

Brooke grimaced, touching the back of her jeans. "I've been sitting in a car for two days. If you don't mind, I'll just stand."

Jessica laughed and picked up a set of keys from the desk, holding them as if reluctant to let them go. Her smile quickly turned to concern. "The electricity and water are on, like you requested. But you won't get phone service before next week." She paused. "You know, I told you we haven't been able to rent it out in a couple of years."

"You said it was damaged by a hurricane." Brooke suddenly felt a stab of concern in the pit of her stomach. "But it is habitable?"

"Well, yes, habitable," Jessica agreed, glancing away as if she couldn't quite meet Brooke's eyes. "But that's not recommended until repairs are made."

"I'll check it out," Brooke said, holding out her hand for the keys.

Jessica reluctantly laid the keys in Brooke's palm. Then she picked up an invoice. "Here's what you owe for yard work."

Brooke gulped, looking at the bill. Would the bills never stop? Never be paid off? All she'd done for the past year was try and settle bills. Bruce had a substantial insurance policy, but he'd also run up substantial bills, having lived beyond his means. She'd lost the big house and big car. After paying creditors, she'd put aside the rest for her and Ben to live on until she could begin to make a living.

With nervous fingers, she opened her purse and took out the checkbook. But she mustn't think about finances right now—just concentrate on one day at a time.

Jessica took the check and thanked her. "I can recommend some motels, if you like."

"Thanks," Brooke said with more confidence than she felt. "But if I can find at least a corner where Ben and I can lay our heads, we'll make out just fine."

Brooke put her arms around her little boy and pulled him close. He looked up at her and they shared an affectionate smile.

Jessica stared after Brooke and Ben as they left the office. When she felt sure they were out of earshot, she picked up the phone and punched some numbers.

"Jake," she said, "I thought you'd want to know. Mrs. Haddon just picked up the keys to the cottage at 26 Seabreeze Lane. She has a little boy, and that cottage is in desperate need of repairs. Nothing's been done to it since the hurricane hit. I think she's really going to need your help."

two

"This is Seabreeze Lane," Brooke commented as she read the street sign, turned the corner, and slowed the car. Seven years ago, the cottages had looked similar, but she'd had eyes only for Bruce—not for cottages. "Help me find number six."

"I think it's this one," Ben said, seeing a little white terrier running toward the road as if preparing to chase the slow-moving vehicle. "Can we keep the dog?"

Brooke glanced at the dog, now wagging its tail and barking a friendly welcome. "It's cute, but obviously belongs to someone." She didn't want to squelch his exuberance by adding that she was concerned about feeding the two of them—she certainly couldn't take on another mouth! "Anyway, the house sits farther back from the road than these."

"I like that one," Ben said. "This one's okay too."

Brooke felt a pang of guilt, knowing Ben was trying to encourage her. He'd done that ever since he'd caught her crying to her mother about the events of the past year since Bruce died. She had no job skills and an almost depleted checkbook. But, she forced a blessing-thought that at least they had the promise of a roof over their heads. Fortunately for them, the Haddons had purchased the cottage years ago, before prices skyrocketed, and had paid it off. Now, the older couple had no need of it since their many travels took them abroad.

"Oh neat, Mom!" Ben exclaimed when Brooke turned down a short winding drive and pulled up beside the cottage, which looked much smaller than she remembered. Ben was out of his seat belt and opening the car door by the time she got the key out of the ignition.

Definitely neat, Brooke was thinking. *If you don't mind a little picket fence with half the slats missing. If you don't mind part of the roof hanging down at the left corner of the house and the banister broken off beneath it. If you don't mind a gutter sticking out precariously from the eaves, or boards in bad need of repair and paint.*

When she'd come here seven years ago, this was a honeymoon cottage. Now it felt like a last resort.

Ben ran up on the porch and plopped down in a swing hanging from a rusty chain hooked to the ceiling, before she could do more than call, "Be careful, Ben." She breathed a sigh of relief when he began to swing without its falling down, bringing the roof with it.

"Listen," Ben admonished.

Brooke smiled and nodded. "Has a real nice squeak," she said, but she wouldn't dare chance sitting on it. It was too late to mention the peeling paint and seat streaked with gritty sand.

The realtor had reminded her more than once that the cottage needed repairs. She should have considered herself warned, nevertheless, unprepared, she reached for the screen door, yelped, and jumped back when it came loose at the top, swinging back and forth like it might topple any minute. "Don't get close," she warned Ben, who'd laughed at her yelping, then looked unconcerned and kept stretching his leg so his foot could swing that squeaky contraption.

Seeing several broken windows, Brooke wondered, *Why bother with a key?* Nevertheless, with fear and trembling, she tried the key in the lock. It turned—maybe too easily. How difficult would it be for an intruder to jiggle that lock? Then she mentally laughed at herself. With all the broken windows, an intruder wouldn't need to jiggle a lock. Cautiously opening the door, she entered precariously, allowing her eyes to adjust to the dimly lit room. Assailing her nostrils was the musty, moldy odor of something having sat in water for a long time. Now she understood why the realtor had been unable to rent it on this resort island. This cottage was a shambles.

Ben was beside her now, pulling on her hand. "Come on, Mom. Let's go in."

"Slowly," Brooke cautioned.

She felt for and flipped a light switch. Nothing changed. "Well, the sound of the floor matches the squeak of the swing," she said with a false brightness as the floorboards creaked with her every step. Ben laughed as he found a particular spot that squeaked and creaked, and he began to rock back and forth on it.

Brooke pushed aside the drapes at the front window, recognizing them as the same ones that had hung there seven years ago. She'd stood in that very spot watching and waiting for Bruce, then feeling swept with joy when he appeared, so handsome, so confident. She'd felt so lucky, so blessed. Why had it gone so wrong? As soon as she asked, an answering thought threatened, and she felt the drape tear in her grasp. She let go. The fading evening light revealed a lining that was thin and worn.

Honeymoon cottage—now as changed and dilapidated as her failed marriage. At least this physical structure could be fixed up, if one had the time, the expertise, and the money. What about her broken life? How could that be fixed—especially in the house that was a constant reminder of pain, heartache, and failure?

Mentally reprimanding herself for indulging in memories best forgotten, Brooke felt her way through the shadowed house. She tried the lamp switches, but no light! She found two light bulbs that worked. One in a bedroom and one in the kitchen. "At least it's furnished," she said, trying to be positive, but her negative self added, *Yeah, furnished with mildew, damp furniture, broken windows, and two light bulbs*.

"Ah, another light," she exclaimed with irony as Ben opened the refrigerator door to expose empty shelves. "Let's go to the store," she said, realizing that first on the agenda was food, light bulbs, and cleaning supplies. If Ben had food, he could survive the inconveniences. Maybe she could make it presentable enough for them to spend the night here. She couldn't afford to waste precious money on a motel.

"We'll leave the kitchen light on," she commented. "Might be dark when we get back."

Just as she made sure Ben was buckled up in the backseat of the car and was ready herself to jump into the driver's seat, a dark blue truck drove up. The driver leaned out the window, his muscular brown arm across the door. "Evening, ma'am," said a deep voice with a southern drawl.

"Evening," Brooke replied, wondering if he was a neighbor.

"Jake Randolph here," he said and hesitated. When Brooke didn't introduce herself, he continued. "I'm a carpenter and want to offer my services." He looked toward the missing corner of the house. "Looks like you could use some help. My prices are the most reasonable you'll find around here."

Before Bruce, Brook might have been swayed by that approach, and "reasonably priced" certainly appealed to her. The man seemed pleasant enough, and looked okay as far as she could make out in the dusk, but she'd learned the hard way that appearances could be deceiving. "I'm in a hurry," she said truthfully. "I'll be glad to take your card."

His grimace matched his words. "Sorry. I didn't bring one with me."

It suddenly dawned on her that she'd warned Ben about talking to strangers. She wasn't setting a very good example. "Well, thanks anyway," she said, opening her car door wider. "I plan to get estimates from local carpenters."

She jumped in and slammed her door before he could say anything more and quickly started the engine. Looking in the rearview mirror as she drove away, she saw the man looking after her. Then he moved back from his window, started his truck, and drove away in the opposite direction.

Frankly, it seemed strange that the most reasonably priced carpenter in the area just happened along as she was moving in. But he did give her his name—if it was his real one. Oh, well, if he meant any harm, her broken windows and flimsy lock were an invitation. Thoughts of him disappeared immediately as her eye moved to the horizon. Dark clouds were blowing in, quickly changing the gray sky to black.

"Let's hurry," she encouraged Ben as she parked at the supermarket. The wind whipped her ponytail around against her cheek as she held onto Ben's hand and hurried to the phone booth beneath the overhang. She made a quick collect call to her parents in Indiana, telling them they'd arrived on the island safely and would call and talk longer after her phone was hooked up.

They wished her well and said to kiss Ben for them.

Brooke led Ben into the store. After buying only the immediate necessities—light bulbs, toilet tissue, cleaning supplies, a mop, milk, cereal, and bread—she made a quick stop at a fast food restaurant to pick up their supper, a rare caloric disaster which Ben considered a treat. Oh well, she could use a few extra pounds, after having lost about ten of them during the past year.

Brooke glanced at the sky, rolling with dark clouds, and saw the palm trees swaying in the wind. She'd remembered sunny days and cloudless skies. Maybe this was just the cloud that had followed her for the past few years. Immediately she reprimanded herself for that attitude. Those years had yielded Ben! The most wonderful blessing one could have. She smiled, remembering her mom's saying, "Good comes from the worst of things."

Full darkness had come and the wind blew strongly by the time they arrived back at the cottage. Brooke replaced a bulb in a living-room lamp, then switched it off. A light shining from that gaping hole in the corner would be an invitation for all sorts of flying creatures. After they ate in the kitchen, Ben began to yawn. For the past two nights he'd been up past his bedtime. She would let him stay up a little longer, so he wouldn't be awake before dawn. She needed her own rest too.

Ben held a chair while Brooke climbed up and changed the burned-out bulb in the bedroom. She preferred not to sleep in the bed where she and Bruce had slept. Already, she felt haunted by ghostly memories.

She stripped Ben's bed but found only moldy sheets in a closet. The blankets, stored in plastic bags, were permeated with a damp, musty odor but at least didn't have black spots like the sheets. They'd just have to sleep without sheets.

She didn't bother bathing Ben because the bathtub was in worse shape than a little boy who hadn't bathed in two days. He resorted to reading the books he'd brought with them on the trip, then fell into a deep sleep with a book over his face.

Brooke washed away the surface grit and grime from the kitchen table, counter top, and appliances, deciding to do deep cleaning, one room at a time, in the daylight. Finally, around midnight, she could keep her eyes open no longer. After washing off, she turned out the light, shucked out of her jeans, and climbed into bed beside Ben. While hearing the wind whistling around the eaves of the little cottage, she thought of the missing corner and broken window panes. Her last coherent thought was, *Oh please, don't rain.*

It rained.

three

In the middle of the night Brooke awakened to the sound of a storm that seemed to be just on the other side of the bedroom wall. Rushing into the living room, with the hall light behind her, she switched on the lamp and viewed an uncanny sight. The wind was whistling through the blinds, and the rain was blowing in through the broken front window, soaking the drapes and sprinkling the armchair.

She shoved the chair into the center of the room. A piece of cardboard box might cover the hole in the window, but she had no tape. She didn't even have a hammer or nail.

At least she found a use for the moldy sheets. After running to get them, piled in the kitchen as trash, she lay them in the corner to soak up the water running down the wall onto the carpet. So that's where the moldy, musty odor came from! That was a revelation, but what to do about it?

"Mommie? What's wrong?"

Brooke, on her hands and knees, turned to see Ben behind her, blinking his sleepy eyes. "Oh, it's just the rain blowing in." She laughed to keep from crying. She mustn't cry. The cottage was saturated with enough water already! She rose from the soggy floor. "Let's see how things are in the other rooms."

After a quick inspection, she saw that everything appeared dry, but the dark spot on the kitchen ceiling looked larger and wet, as if water were up there just waiting to find a hole, and it might even make its own. She sighed helplessly. "Let's go back to bed."

She and Ben snuggled beneath the blanket. She could pray. But she couldn't ask for anything. She'd had "everything," and it had only brought misery. *I'll count my blessings,* Brooke reminded herself, forcing her mind away from disturbing thoughts. *Thank You, Lord, that I have my son. Help me to be able to make a secure home for him—here in this "last resort" kind of place. I'm trying—but I'm scared.*

⮞

Brooke was out of bed before the soft morning light drifted through the cracked window, exposing the torn curtain, dirty floor, and peeling paint. Then she turned her attention to the grimy night table beside the four-poster bed where a precious little boy lay breathing easily through parted lips. A blanket twisted tightly around him except for one arm that was flung out on her side of the bed. Maybe that's what had awakened her.

Blessing, blessing, she reminded herself and smiled at her precious boy. God had let her keep the most important part of her life. She must learn how to be grateful. With that determination she headed for the kitchen and ate a bowl of cereal while looking out upon the small back yard, filled with puddles, surrounded by pieces of a broken picket fence. Who was it who said it's better to live in a corner of an attic rather than in mansion with a cranky woman?

Oh, yes, that was from the Bible—Proverbs, she thought.

Well, she'd try not to be cranky, but more and more she felt like the old woman who lived in a shoe with so many children she didn't know what to do. At least the old woman was able to spank her children and put them to bed. Brooke didn't have a passel of children, but still, she hardly knew what to do. She had to try, so she began by dragging the wet sheets outside and stuffing them into a metal trash can.

Ben came into the kitchen while she was washing the grime off her hands. "It's not raining in the living room anymore," he said, looking disappointed. Then he brightened. "But the floor's still squishy. It feels neat to jump on it. You wanna do it, Mom?"

Brooke laughed. Leave it to Ben find something positive. "Not right now," she said. "You need to eat breakfast. We have a lot of things to do today." She poured his cereal and milk into a bowl, one of the few dishes she'd found in the cupboard.

Just then bells began to ring. The clear notes resounded and vibrated as if waking up the landscape and sending a musical message across the morning sky. It had a similar effect deep within her soul.

"What's that sound?" Ben asked, his spoon poised above his bowl.

"Church bells," Brooke said contemplatively, realizing that she hadn't heard church bells ring since she and Bruce had been on this island seven years ago. It had a nice sound, as if saying that God is alive and well. At the same time she felt slightly guilty. She'd resolved to get Ben in church even though so many things in her own life remained unresolved. The guilt increased when he asked excitedly, "Can we go and see the bells?"

No way could they go to church. Clothes were still crunched up in boxes in the trunk of the car. There was so much to do. "Not today," she said and, seeing his downcast countenance, she added, "But we can read a Bible story." Then she remembered the Bible, too, was packed away somewhere.

"Okay," he said. He took a big bite of cereal, then with milk running down his chin, jumped out of his chair and ran from the room.

In an instant, he returned with one of his favorite books that her parents had given him for Christmas. "This Bible story," he said.

"Perfect," Brooke said. "Noah and the Flood." She'd read it a million times to him and he knew it by heart now, but it seemed to fit after that watery fiasco of last night. They hadn't drowned, and perhaps the church bells were a reminder that there was somewhere a rainbow. "You eat and I'll read," she said.

Finally, coming to the end, she read, "And Noah took the animals, two by two, into the ark. The birds, the butterflies, the rabbits, the dogs, the cats—"

"It didn't say alligators," he noticed for the first time.

"Well. . .no," Brooke agreed. "But alligators are like whales and fish. They live in water, so they didn't have to be put in the ark."

"Oh, okay," he said, and Brooke realized anew how much this child trusted her. She must teach him the right way. That was a huge responsibility, considering how much she, herself, had to learn.

Ben picked up his bowl and drank the milk. "Can we go to the lagoon and see the alligators?"

There was so much to do. She'd never get done. "Not today, Ben," she said and heard the weariness in her voice and saw the disappointment in his eyes. What could she get done after all? Even if the phone were hooked up, businesses weren't open. She couldn't call around for estimates on repairs. Oh, well. They made it through last night—didn't drown or get swallowed up by some wild beast or get attacked by intruders— and they were none the worse for the grime and dirt. How long would it be before she stopped saying that she didn't have time to do anything that was important to Ben?

"Let's go to the beach," she said impulsively.

"Yea!" he shrieked and ran to her, throwing his arms around her, almost knocking the chair over.

Brooke laughed. This little boy didn't need a clean cottage nearly as much as he needed a mother to spend time with him. She hugged him, then admonished, "Get your clothes on. What you wore yesterday will be fine."

"Can I go barefoot?" he called as he struck out across the kitchen.

"Put your tennis shoes on. We'll walk. It's not far."

The few blocks to the beach turned out to be a little farther than Brooke remembered, however the crisp morning breeze and warm sunlight felt wonderful on her skin. She tried to ignore the fact that people in cars were going in the opposite direction, probably on their way to church. At least she could remind Ben that God was in nature.

"God created such a beautiful world, didn't He, Ben?" she commented as the public beach came into view.

"Yeah," he agreed. "I can't even see the end of it."

"Hey, you're right," she said, looking where the horizon should be; however, the ocean blended with the heavens. In Indiana, the eyesight would be stopped by city building, community houses, or a forest of trees against the sky. "It looks as if you can see forever."

"Yeah, and I never saw white sand before." He scooped up handfuls and let it sift through his fingers. Then he stood still, his eyes wide, listening.

She heard it. The sound of yelping puppies.

"Oh, Mom, cum'on!" Ben pulled on her hand, leading her down the beach toward a crowd of people.

Going closer, Brooke saw a young couple in folding chairs behind a cardboard box. Ben rushed up to join other children, while adults looked on with smiling faces.

"Can I have a puppy?" Ben asked loudly, and it seemed to Brooke that everyone looked at her for the answer, as expectant as Ben. Then she saw the sign on the box: "Free Puppies."

She walked closer and peered into the box. That was a mistake, because the puppies were absolutely adorable. "What kind are they?" she asked.

"The mother is a miniature Japanese Spitz," said the young man in the folding chair as he held his hand about six inches off the ground. "We're not sure about the male."

The young woman spoke up. "The female is our dog. The male could be our neighbor's dog that got out of its fence or a black mutt that wandered into our back yard a while back. So. . ." She shrugged.

Brooke could see that the puppies were a mixture of colors. Ben picked up one that was coal black with a spot of white on the back of his neck and a streak of white beneath his mouth and down along his chest. "Oh," he exclaimed, spying another. "I want to see that one."

Brooke leaned closer and saw a coal-black ball of fur curled up in the corner. It was so fuzzy she couldn't even tell where its face was. Apparently the young man couldn't either, for when he picked it up, its bushy little tail faced the group. He turned it around and set it on the ground.

The onlookers, including Brooke, gasped at the adorable puppy face surrounded with a thick mane of hair, reminding her of a lion or, she realized more accurately, a werewolf.

The puppy shook itself, lifted its tail and its head, and waddled across the sand as if it owned the world. Its tail was longer than its legs. The legs were so short, its tummy scraped across little piles of sand, making a groove. Everyone laughed, so intrigued they didn't make a move until the puppy began to scoot closer to the ocean.

"I'll get it," Ben shouted and began to run.

The puppy ran faster but Ben caught it at the ocean's edge and swept it up into his arms. He brought the squirming puppy back to the group but wouldn't let go. "I saved its life, Mom. Just like Noah did."

While he was pleading, "Can I keep it? Please," Brooke had visions of shots, visits to the vet, dog food. At least it was male, so she wouldn't have to worry about a slew of little puppies.

"How big will he get?" she asked.

"Mitzi weighs twelve pounds," the young man said. "So, I'd say this one shouldn't get over. . .say fourteen, fifteen pounds."

It wouldn't eat much at that weight. Maybe she could cut corners elsewhere. Ben had no dad, no friends, and was without his maternal grandparents who had doted on him. This puppy could be a friend to Ben and maybe free her up to do her chores. He'd become like glue since Bruce died, as if afraid something might happen to her.

Looking at Ben and the puppy, she doubted she could pry them apart with a crowbar. "Okay," she said.

His little face simply glowed with delight, and he nuzzled the puppy's fur with his chin. Then his big brown eyes rolled up to hers. "Can I have two—like Noah?"

Brooke gasped. "That's where I draw the line!" The onlookers laughed. "Come on, young man," she admonished and they headed on down the beach, Ben hugging the little critter. He looked up. "Thanks, Mom. I really knew I couldn't have another one. I love this one. I really love him."

Brooke touched his shoulder. Yes, she'd cut corners or maybe plug that missing corner of the living room with old boards if that's what it took to make her son happy.

four

Early Monday morning, Brooke and Ben were out back feeding the puppy a bowl of milk. "We're going to have to teach him to stay outside," Brooke told him. Last night she'd said the puppy could stay in a box in the kitchen, but the whimpering threatened to last all night, so she'd finally consented to bringing the box into the bedroom. That had satisfied both Ben and the puppy.

"You two play for awhile," she said needlessly, remembering that Ben and the dog had been content with each other for most of Sunday, while she worked on the house and even got the bathroom into decent living condition. Now, in shorts, T-shirt, and tennis shoes, she was ready to tackle that impossible cottage again.

"Pardon me, ma'am," she heard and turned with a start toward the voice. A man came striding across the yard toward her. "I knocked but nobody answered," he explained. "The car was out front, so I thought you might be back here. I'm Jake Randolph."

That truck driver! Should she shake his hand? What did he want? Maybe he was a neighbor being friendly. No, Saturday night he drove away. "I'm. . ." She hesitated, not wanting to be impolite, yet not wanting to be too familiar. "I'm Mrs. Haddon."

"Yes, ma'am," he said in that friendly drawl of Saturday night. Definitely a southerner. "My friend Jessica Lawler said you'd moved in and could use some repairs."

She knew Jessica Lawler was the realtor and nodded briefly for him to continue.

"I'm here to offer my services. I'm a carpenter."

"Thanks for stopping by," Brooke said, uncertain about this persistent man claiming to be a carpenter. He did look the part, being bronzed by the sun and with sun-bleached golden highlights through his brown hair. Also, in jeans and T-shirt, he looked to be in great physical condition and quite muscular. But if he were good at his trade, would he be running around begging for work like this? She thought not. "I plan to ask around, maybe get some estimates and then make my decision. If you want to leave a card—"

"I do have one this time," he said and laughed lightly, as if embarrassed that he hadn't had one on Saturday night. "However," he continued with a wry smile as he moved his hand to the back pocket of his jeans. "I do better than offer a card. To prove my worth, I always make at least one small repair free of charge."

Brooke's gray-green eyes locked with his warm brown ones for an instant before she quickly lowered her gaze to the card he offered. That instant was long enough to see a flush begin on his bronzed face as if he knew what she was thinking.

She stared at the card. *Puppies might be free*, she was thinking, *but not some carpenter's services! Free? Ha! He might hammer a nail in somewhere and then try to sell her vinyl siding or a new roof or new windows.*

"How did you manage during that storm Saturday night?" he asked. "I notice your corner is missing."

Real observant, there! With a slight lift to her chin, she avoided his eyes. She'd prefer he leave before she had to demand it. "We. . .managed."

"I'm glad to hear it," he said, then walked over to Ben,

who was offering the puppy a stick, then pulling it away when the puppy tried to bite it. "Hi, Buddy. I'm Jake." He stooped down.

"I'm not Buddy. I'm Ben." The two laughed together, but Brooke's motherly protective instincts surfaced, seeing Ben welcome Jake as if they were long-time friends—even let him pet his puppy.

"Look at that purple tongue. Looks like you've got a little Chow here."

"Yeah, I saved his life," Ben said proudly.

Jake, on eye-level with Ben, remarked, "Well son, according to an old Chinese proverb, that means you're responsible for him all his life."

Ben's eyes were big and round, basking in the man's attention. "He was going to drown in the ocean."

"That's a slight exaggeration, Ben," Brooke admonished, wondering if he got that from his politician father too.

The man grinned, like he was amused at the exaggeration. "Have you named him?"

Ben nodded, his dark eyes gazing trustingly into the eyes of the stranger. "Taz." he said.

That was the first Brooke had heard of that! Ben had simply been calling him "Puppy." She hadn't known it was a Chow either, but now that Jake mentioned it, she'd heard or read that Chows have purple tongues.

"Taz," the man mused and glanced up quickly at Brooke. "Like the cartoon character?"

"Yeah," Ben said. "He's neat."

Ben thinks the Tasmanian Devil is neat! He also seemed to think this stranger was neat. The cartoon character might look neat with those rather innocent eyes, his tongue hanging out, and that cute laugh, but inside he was an out-of-control, wild, crazy thing. This man kneeling in front of her son looked rather neat too, with that quick smile over perfect white teeth in a ruggedly-handsome tanned face with little laugh lines at his mouth and eyes, as if he laughed a lot. But who could trust what might be lurking inside that neat exterior?

She studied the card for a moment. It looked authentic. "Randolph Construction," it read. Under that was Jake's name, an address, and phone number. She was tempted to ask him to look at the corner of the house, but she'd trusted better looking men than this—her late husband, in fact—and where did that get her? No, she simply could not take a person at face value.

"Thank you for stopping by, Mr. Randolph," she said abruptly. She couldn't stand here all day. "I'll get back to you if I need your services."

Jake immediately rose from his kneeling position near Ben and the puppy. "I understand," he said, color coming to his face. "I shouldn't have barged in. I should have explained—"

"No," she said, uncertain about the whole situation. "I just don't like people coming to my door, selling things, or making offers."

Ben came over, holding the puppy beneath its arms, exposing its belly, the only spot that wasn't covered with thick black hair. "Yeah," he said. "One time this man said he was going to give us a million dollars worth of groceries."

"A thousand, darling," Brooke corrected.

"Well, lots of groceries. A whole room full and Mom asked why and he said he wanted to come in and vacuum the carpets." Ben snorted and shook his head, his eyes wide. "Mom said no."

"I see," Jake said. "And your mom was right. You should never let strangers in the house, and I should never have approached you this way." His brown eyes looked truly repentant as he glanced from Ben to Brooke. "When Jessica called and said a woman and her son moved in, she told me of the damage."

Did she also tell him that she had no husband—that there wasn't a man around? "Thank you again, Mr. Randolph," Brooke said, trying not to be fooled by this now-contrite, apologetic, seemingly-trustworthy, helpful man. How many of those were in the world anyway? *Something for nothing? Ha! That'll be the day!* "I will let Jessica know if I need your services."

"I realize I should have had Jessica Lawler contact you," Jake said and laughed uncomfortably. "Sorry I bothered you. Do contact Jessica, please." Brooke noticed that he was walking rather sideways then, as if afraid of her. What was this man's problem?

❧

"Good-bye, Ben. Bye, Taz. Good-bye—" Jake hesitated, realizing she hadn't given her first name. Jessica had said the Haddons moved in. He nodded and added, "Mrs. Haddon."

"Good-bye," she said, and the word sounded final. He knew, without a doubt, there was no way this woman was going to call for his help. How did it go wrong? It never had before. It must have been his showing up Saturday night, then appearing today. Or was it that she was more distrusting than anyone else he'd ever approached? Or perhaps there was no Mr. Haddon, and she was being particularly cautious.

Whatever, she obviously wasn't accustomed to having someone come by and offer to help. Now how was he going to get himself out of this? He spread his hands and began backing away. "I'll try and approach this in a different manner."

She didn't return his smile, and her dismissing gaze

plainly said, "Don't bother." He'd better get out while he could. He felt certain that if he showed up here again, she'd call the police. He didn't need that. An accusation, founded or not, could prove to be disastrous in his situation. Even something as simple as a call to the Better Business Bureau could reach his parole officer and land him right back in federal prison.

five

Brooke tried to dismiss the incident with the man claiming to be a carpenter, but she couldn't get it off her mind as she went about the process of cleaning and throwing away. The next-door neighbors on the left, a young couple, left before eight o'clock, apparently going off to work. An older couple, on the right, came over just to introduce themselves as Mary and Frank Lee and give advice about trash pickup. Brooke asked about getting the corner of the house repaired, and they mentioned a couple of construction companies that might be able to help, but there was no mention of a Jake Randolph.

"Less expensive if you can get somebody that knows a little about carpentry," Frank informed her.

Brooke nodded. Would that be Jake Randolph?

She didn't know whether to be proud of herself for having expelled a ne'er-do-well, or whether to be ashamed that she'd turned away well-needed "free" assistance.

But no! She could not chance endangering herself or Ben.

At least the adrenaline was flowing, and that spurred her on with the cleaning. She even engaged Ben in some of it.

The air was humid, she was hot and sweaty, Ben wanted a popsicle, and she said it was too close to suppertime and decided to stop for awhile. Just as she poked her head in the refrigerator, basking in the coolness that touched her face and trying to decide what to do for supper, a knock sounded on the door.

She straightened immediately, slammed the door shut, and

stiffened. *Oh, surely, not that man again! Where was Ben.* "Ben?" she called.

"I'm out here," he said, his voice coming from right outside the back screen door, where he often played when she wanted him to stay nearby.

"Just stay where you are," she said and guardedly walked through the kitchen, the small foyer between the other rooms in the center of the cottage, and through the living room. If the person at the door was Jake, she would slam the front door and lock it, then run and get Ben and lock the back door. If he tried to open the front screen door, it would probably surprise him as it had her, by hanging on its lower hinge only.

Guardedly, she approached the door. A sigh of relief escaped her, and she cautioned her erratic heartbeat to calm down when she saw a pretty woman with short auburn curls, friendly brown eyes, and a light sprinkling of freckles across her nose, holding a box. Three stair-step boys stood with her, each holding something in his hands. A late model SUV was parked in the driveway.

"Hi, I'm Ginger, from a church down the way. Hope you haven't had supper."

"No," Brooke said, half laughing with relief and as surprised as when Jake had showed up, but more trusting of this woman with children from a church. Surely they weren't out to poison her. "Watch out for the screen. It might fall on you."

They stepped aside while Brooke opened the door slightly, then put her hands near the top to open it wider. "I should just take this thing off," she apologized.

"If you have children like mine, you should," Ginger agreed. "These kids broke me with buying new screens.

They don't know how to push on the wooden part. Finally, I decided to quit fussin' and live with holey screens. 'Course, we do get quite a few flies."

Brooke had no idea how much of this was exaggeration, but both women laughed as Ginger and the three boys paraded through the house to the kitchen. Brooke called Ben inside.

The woman introduced herself again. "I'm Ginger Harris. This is Mike and he's ten, George, eight, and Danny, five."

"I'm five," Ben piped up. Brooke introduced herself and Ben. She'd have to question Ginger about school in the fall. But for now, Ginger had set the box on the table and was taking off a towel. "Spaghetti, anyone?" she asked.

"Yeah," Ben said, along with Ginger's children.

"Okay if we eat with you?" Ginger asked.

Brooke laughed. "Shouldn't that be my question, since it's your food?"

"Nope, it's your food. We cooked it for you."

All the children beamed as if they'd played a huge part in it—and enjoyed themselves.

"This is so thoughtful," Brooke said, feeling slightly embarrassed that all the dishes, pots, and pans were out on her counter tops. But at least the kitchen table was clean. "Are you a neighbor?"

Only the slightest pause ensued as Ginger continued taking the dishes out of the box. "Got a microwave?" she asked.

"That I do have!" Brooke replied. She put the dish of sauce in it and punched the buttons.

"Who is my neighbor?" Ginger asked, tilting her head and sort of looking toward the ceiling. Brooke recognized the phrase as something in the Bible. Maybe it was Jesus who asked, "Who is your neighbor?" and the answer was that we all should be neighbors, Good Samaritans, brothers and sisters in Christ.

Brooke nodded, seeing the gleam in Ginger's eyes, and she felt as if her spirit were communicating with this woman. Maybe she could accept friendship from her. "Okay," Brooke conceded, "we're neighbors. Now, do you live on this street?"

"No," Ginger said and avoided Brooke's eyes. "You forgot about the napkins, kids. Who wants to place them?"

"I will," George offered immediately, as Mike stuck out his hand, then withdrew it in deference to his brother. These children really wanted to be a part of this. How wonderful if she could teach this attitude to Ben. He and Danny were near the back door with the puppy, already totally accepting of one another.

Ginger's next glance at Brooke, who was watching her closely, held a note of concern, but she smiled. "We'll get to particulars later, okay?" She turned toward the boys. "Okay, wash your hands."

Brooke was glad to see that Ben put Taz in his box and ran along behind the other children to the bathroom. If he hated anything, it was to wash his hands. Ginger reached into the box and brought out a plate. Wow! She'd even brought brownies.

The microwave beeped. "Soup's on!" Ginger called.

"I thought we were having spaghetti," quipped Mike, coming into the kitchen. He and his mom exchanged an affectionate gaze, before Ginger reached over and mussed his hair.

"Okay, who wants to say the blessing?" Ginger asked after the other children gathered round.

"Me. Me. Me," came the replies in unison from Ginger's children, following by Ben's weaker "Me" that sounded like a question.

"Maybe we should let Ben say it," Ginger said, "since it's his house."

They all looked at him. He thrust out his hands, like he and Brooke were accustomed to doing together. They all held hands. Brooke wondered what he'd say. He hadn't prayed before in front of anyone but her and her parents. She watched him through her lashes.

"Mmmm. God bless Mommy and my doggie and the buh-sketti." He moved his hands out of the others and spread them. "That's all."

"Amen," Brooke and Ginger said, then smiled while the children giggled until Ginger cast them a warning glance.

Everyone dug in. Brooke thought the food delicious, and the others wasted no time eating. The conversation was about children, school, the area, but nothing personal. Ginger's asking no personal questions pleased Brooke. She was curious about Ginger, but didn't ask, lest she would have to reciprocate by revealing her own personal life. She didn't know if she wanted to do that just yet.

After they finished, Ginger said, "I'll do the dishes tonight, kids. Your turn tomorrow night."

"You always say that when we eat off paper plates," Mike said with clear affection for his mother.

"You've got to get up early in the morning to be quicker than me," Ginger said pointedly to her son. She turned to Brooke. "Where's your trash can?"

"There and there and there and there," Brooke replied, pointing at plastic grocery bags placed around the kitchen.

Ginger made eye contact with her boys. "You guys know what to do."

They each took their plates and put them into the trash. "We don't throw away our silverware," Ginger joked about the plastic forks. She filled the sink with sudsy water and put the forks in. "If you want the leftovers, you can put them in something, and I'll wash out my dishes. Now, you kids run outside."

While the two women worked together with the food and clean up, coffee was brewing.

"Your children are so well-behaved," Brooke complimented.

"Thank the Lord," Ginger replied, and Brooke knew that was not a trite phase.

"I'm a single parent," Ginger explained. "My husband walked out on us while I was pregnant with Danny. It was hard to cope with being a single mother, and I couldn't have done it without my family and their reminding me that God can work in and change even the worst situations."

Brooke nodded. She didn't know how that might work for her. She didn't have the faith that it would—only the hope that it would. The phrase, "Oh, ye of little faith," crossed her mind, and she knew it applied to herself.

"I need to hear things like that," Brooke admitted. She asked, as if joking, "Did God send you to me?"

Ginger gazed at Brooke for a long moment. "God. . . ," she said, then added soberly, "and Jake."

six

Brooke felt like the breath had been knocked out of her. What was going on here? "You know. . .Jake?" Maybe this was Jake's wife and children, and he was legitimate after all. She sat down in a kitchen chair.

Ginger dried her hands and sat opposite her. "I've known Jake all my life. After my husband left, I had a rough time. It's easier now, since Jake moved in with me."

Brooke regretted that her intake of breath was audible. Her immediate emotion was that this divorced woman and a man lived together—apparently with children in the house.

Oh, how judgmental! This woman was being a good neighbor—regardless of her personal situation. She was obviously an excellent mother with children who adored her. She gave every indication that she was a Christian. But so had Bruce—and Brooke didn't want to think of Bruce just now, nor ever.

And who am I to judge? I am in the aftermath of a failed marriage. Perhaps my sins were not of overt commission but omission. Is that any more excusable?

Then, making Brooke's thoughts even worse, Ginger said quietly, "I'm Jake's sister."

This was unbelievable!

"Did he send you here?" Brooke asked, wondering if she should be glad or upset.

"Oh, no. He wouldn't send me out to repair any damage he's done." Ginger laughed, realizing what she'd said. "He

35

does his own repairs—he's in that business, you know." Her expression grew serious. "But after he told me he hadn't approached you in a businesslike matter, I just didn't want you to have the wrong impression of him. And he's not begging for work, believe me."

Shaking her head, Brooke didn't know how to apologize. "He was very nice," she said. "I'm the problem. Right now, my trust-quotient with men is at an all-time low."

Ginger snorted. "Tell me about it!" she said, understanding. "When a man walks out on a wife and three kids, you never even want to look at one again." She grinned, and a wee gleam appeared in her eyes. "Well, almost never."

Brooke couldn't help but smile. She really liked Ginger. "I understand that. My husband stepped out on me during our marriage. He died a year ago. But all that's no excuse to treat your brother so rudely."

"He understands. And he really would like to repair that corner in your living room free of charge." She lifted her hand. "Oh, I know what you're thinking—nothing's free, right? But that's not the case here. And if you want, we'll come with him."

Apologetic, Brook told her that wasn't necessary. "But I'd like for you to come."

"Great," Ginger said, smiling broadly. "If you don't mind, we will. It's good for the kids to make new friends." She looked toward the back yard. "They love that puppy."

Brooke told her how they'd acquired the puppy. "I just couldn't refuse Ben, especially after he put the Noah guilt trip on me."

Ginger laughed. "They know how to work us, but I'm not taking on an animal. They'll all be in school in a few months, and I'm looking forward to a little peace and quiet. Oh, speaking of school," she said, "Ben and Danny might be going to school together since they're the same age. There are no children Danny's age around our house. They're either older or younger or their families come here only for vacations. He and Ben have really taken to each other."

"It's helpful to me for them to play together," Brooke assured her. "I don't want to impose, but you're welcome to come over and bring the children any time."

"Great! I'll stop by and let you know when Jake can do the job."

"Okay, but supper's on me," Brook insisted. "That is, if you don't mind sandwiches."

"A staple at our house," Ginger said.

"Any preferences?"

"Yeah," Ginger said. "We'll eat anything that doesn't bite us first." She laughed at her own joke, then screwed up her face. "Except the boys can't stand the salad type—you know, egg salad, chicken salad. They like the solid kind, like bologna or ham. Peanut butter's fine too."

"I can handle that," Brooke said confidently.

≈

Although Ben was anxious to see his new friends again, Brooke was glad to have the next few days to herself, Ben, and Taz. She took Taz to the vet for his shots and then spent over an hour finding just the right collar—a bright red strip with shiny rhinestones. When they got home and she fastened the beautiful new collar, it promptly sank into the mane of thick fur around the dog's neck and was completely hidden.

She made a dent in her deep cleaning, bought new sheets and curtains for her bedroom, and discovered at night she fell into an exhausted sleep, with hardly a thought of Bruce.

Early Friday morning Ginger stopped by to say Jake could

start on the corner that evening and to confirm that supper was still on. Brooke and Ben went to the store to buy peanut butter, jelly, bread, lunch meat, lettuce, tomato, cucumbers, potato chips, a bag of chocolate chip cookies, and a bag of oatmeal raisin cookies.

Brooke dreaded seeing Jake again, wondering if she should be apologetic or what. He and his sister seemed so good and helpful, but outward appearances could be deceiving.

It was after five, with a few hours of light left, when Ginger drove up in her SUV and parked in the driveway. The blue truck pulled in behind her. While greeting Ginger and the children, Brooke's peripheral vision observed Jake getting equipment from the back of the truck.

Brooke carefully held the screen while Ginger and her brood filed in. By that time Jake was heading toward the corner of the house with a ladder. She needn't have worried about what to say. He looked her way, nodded once, and commented, "Looks like that screen could use a little fixin' too," then continued on. Before she had time to think about conversation with Jake, Ginger and the children were crowding in around her. Brooke already had the lettuce leaves separated, the tomatoes sliced, lunch meat on a plate in the refrigerator, and the paper plates and napkins on the table.

"Okay, give me your clean hands," Ginger instructed her boys, and they all held hands. Brooke and Ben completed the circle, and Ginger gave thanks for new friends and the food.

After she finished, Brooke asked, "Would your brother like to join us?"

"He wouldn't know how to sit down and eat! That guy's on the run all the time. I'll take him something."

Feeling embarrassed, Brooke insisted, "He's welcome."

"He'd rather eat while he works."

"It's really my. . ." She looked around at the children, each fixing their own sandwiches expertly and reminded herself she'd have to teach Ben to be more independent as she fixed his sandwich for him. "It's my attitude, isn't it?" she added finally.

"No. You were perfectly right. He simply hadn't thought about how his cheap and free offers might look to you."

"I want to at least invite him in," Brooke said. She handed Ben his sandwich, then headed for the front door.

She was so intent upon doing the right thing that she completely forgot the front screen, pushed on it, and nearly fell on her face, squealing as she tried to balance her feet and the door at the same time. Chagrined at her inability to even make a simple request of a man she had insulted, while at the same time telling herself she was right because he had been a stranger, she mumbled reprimands to herself.

Just as she neared the corner, a head stuck out from over the roof. Brooke jumped back. She caught herself on the swing, and it squeaked, moving back, taking her with it. She almost lost her balance again.

Jake politely stared down at the ground beneath him, but she felt sure that was a grin playing around his lips and it rather infuriated her. She straightened herself and silently reminded her feet to stay firmly planted on the porch, and after clearing her throat and swallowing, she realized she was again at a loss for words.

She couldn't very well say she was sorry she hadn't accepted a stranger upon first—or second—meeting. She still wasn't sure about him. And he didn't say a word. Was he trying to punish her for rejecting his earlier offer? Then suspicions arose again. Why would he want to come back, after she'd been what he would probably consider rude?

Finding her voice, she spoke in what she hoped was a congenial tone, but it sounded irritated to her. "Would you like to come in for a sandwich? Some sandwiches? Um, something to eat?"

"Thanks," he said quite formally. "I want to try and finish this before dark. You might ask Ginger to wrap me up a sandwich for later."

"Sure," Brooke said, feeling a sense of relief. Something about this man unnerved her. She wasn't sure if it was him or herself. And she knew it was because she had lost her trust in many things—particularly people—after having been duped by an unfaithful husband.

She turned, hearing a movement behind her. Ginger held out a paper plate laden with food. "Here you go," she said.

Brooke took it and immediately knew that was a mistake. She was going to try and hand this up to the roof, while he would try and reach down for it. She'd surely drop it or he would topple on his head. "You want to come down?" she asked.

"Just lay it on the swing," he said. "I'll get it."

seven

Jake didn't want to chance falling on his head, but he did chance leaning over the roof and taking a look at Brooke Haddon when she'd held the plate, about to lift it up to him. She was a natural beauty without even trying, he could easily tell, although she didn't seem to wear a trace of makeup and her blond hair was pulled back in a ponytail.

Her expressive gray-green eyes, fringed with long dark lashes, had held a touch of wariness the first two times he'd seen her. When she'd looked up at him on the roof, however, he'd sensed a trace of warmth in them, matching her thin smile, as if she might decide to give him the benefit of the doubt concerning his character. He felt a sudden emptiness in the pit of his stomach and told himself he'd better go down and devour the sandwiches and keep his mind off both his character and the pretty woman.

While he ate, alone, he did think about what Ginger had told him. Brooke Haddon was a widow whose husband had died a year ago. Having a single sister and being actively involved with the singles at church, he could understand the caution of a mother without a husband around. That would explain her wariness when he approached her about repairs.

She was even sorry if she'd treated him unkindly, Ginger had said, and she'd decided that he could repair the corner of the house. Jake had breathed a great sigh of relief at that. He didn't relish any kind of confrontation or explanation with his parole officer, who wasn't interested in excuses, just adherence to the letter of the law.

Brooke, he thought, with a sense of pleasure. It was a beautiful name, causing him to think of a gently rolling stream in a green pasture. It had a musical quality to it. *I wonder, where did you come from and where are you going, gentle Brooke?*

Jake poked the last bite of sandwich in his mouth and thrust the paper plate down on the swing. *What am I doing?* he asked himself. *I cannot afford the luxury of thinking about a woman as if I'm some young innocent kid just looking for a companionable mate. I'm thirty-five years old, with a past that has its consequences. And I know how temptations can sneak up on a person.*

Knowing he had no excuse for thinking about Brooke Haddon, or any woman, in a way that hinted at a personal relationship, he climbed back onto the roof. How many times did he have to keep giving his personal life to the Lord? He answered that immediately. *As many times as needed!* Fighting back his instant of frustration, he pounded the nails into the wood with renewed vigor.

After finishing the corner and getting the gutter back in place, Jake began to inspect the roof for loose shingles. When he reached the back of the house, Ginger, Mrs. Haddon, and the children were out there. The two women sat in kitchen chairs under a tree, watching the children give bits of bread crust to the puppy.

Jake regretted having to break up that jovial group, but felt impelled to yell down. "Hey, kids. Don't feed that bread to the puppy. He'll get a tummy ache."

"What do we fee him?" Mike yelled back, squinting up toward the evening sun.

"Puppy food."

"We got some, Mom?" Ben inquired.

"No," she said, having intended to feed the dog on table scraps. "We'll get some next time I go to the store." She didn't add that she intended to continue feeding table scraps to the dog. *What people in their right mind would throw food in the garbage when you had a perfectly good animal willing to eat it?*

"Throw a stick," Ginger said. "Teach the dog to fetch."

The dog wasn't as excited about a stick as he was about the bread. If Jake's sister wasn't sitting there with his little nephews, Brooke would inform the man, who apparently thought he had a right to tell her how to raise her dog, that she'd had dogs when she was a child. Every dog she'd ever known ate tables scraps. They didn't go to the vet either, except to get a rabies shot. And they all lived to a ripe old age. Jake should be paying attention to the roof, not little boys playing with a dog.

As if anticipating Brooke's now-somber mood, Ginger explained, "Jake has a friend who runs an obedience school for dogs. He's learned a few things from him."

Brooke nodded. "I don't suppose I should give the poor dog a bone, either."

Ginger grinned. "That's right. Jake says that's as hard on a dog's digestive system as on a human's."

Brooke couldn't imagine separating a dog from his bone. Seeing the movement of Jake standing up on the roof, she saw that he was walking over the ridge, toward the front. "If he's finished, I need to thank him and see what I owe."

Ginger stood. "We need to go too. We'll wear out our welcome."

"No way," Brooke said. "You're welcome anytime. And I

mean that. But my first priority is to get this house in shape."

Ginger smiled. "I'll have you guys over to my place soon. That is, if I can make a pathway through the clutter."

Brooke laughed. "Couldn't be any worse than mine."

"Three boys?" Ginger commented with raised eyebrows, then turned toward the boys. "Okay, you guys. Time to go. Scoot your booties."

She paid no attention as they protested, asked if they could stay a little longer, if Ben could go home with them, if they could have a dog or at least a cat, that they were the only kids in the world without a pet. Finally Ginger began to count, "One—two—three—"

Off they went, running around the side of the house, with Ben and the puppy on their heels.

"You amaze me, Ginger," Brooke said. "I've never seen anyone control their children as easily as you do."

"It hasn't always been that way," she confided. "My husband couldn't discipline himself, and the boys were wild. After Jake came to live with us, he began to discipline them in a teaching way, and it makes life better for all of us. I was indulging them too, because their dad left. Jake said I was doing them no favors by letting them get by with things. They'd turn out to be as irresponsible as my ex. I began to realize he was right. Now they know that if we're going to have fun, we're going to be responsible first. Works better for all of us."

"I think I could learn a lot from you," Brooke said sincerely.

"The most important thing," Ginger said, "is teaching them about God and Jesus. I don't know how people do it without that kind of reference. What do they use as a guideline?"

Brooke nodded. "That's something we neglected 'till I moved back in with my parents. I want to get Ben into Sunday school. That's been neglected for a long time now."

"No time like the present," Ginger said, reminding Brooke of something she'd entirely forgotten. "Sunday is Easter, you know."

eight

When the alarm scared her out of her sleep, Brooke popped up like a jack-in-the-box, staring into the darkness. In an attempt to shut off the offending sound, she only succeeded in knocking the clock off the table. It hit the floor with a dull thud and continued to rattle her brain.

If she hadn't had to nearly stand on her head and roll out of bed to shut off that offending contraption, she'd simply keep her eyes shut and sleep at least until daylight.

But leave it to her trusty watchdog to begin barking and her son to come into the room asking, as if he'd been waiting for this all night, "Is it time to go, Mom?"

"Can you see to turn on the lamp?" she asked.

He did, causing her to close her eyes tightly, then open them slowly. Finally, she stared accusingly at the clock registering 5:30 A.M. That would have been bad enough, but because of Daylight Savings Time, she'd set the clock ahead last night. To her system, the time was only 4:30 A.M.

Had she simply promised Ginger, she would call and say they couldn't make it. But Ben had been looking forward to this. And if she was going to teach her son that Easter was more than bunnies, baskets, eggs, and new clothes, then there was no time like the present to begin. With a groan, she threw back the blanket and smiled faintly at her precious boy who said, "I've never gone to a sunrise in my life, Mom. I'm real 'cited."

Pushing back her hair from her face, a faint smile was all

Brooke could manage at this early moment. Yes, Ben was excited about going to church on the beach. And she felt reasonably sure it wouldn't hurt her, either—if she could stay awake for it.

❧

When Brooke pulled into the church parking lot, Jake stood near the entrance. She wondered if he were the assigned parking attendant for the morning. Surely he wasn't waiting just for her. She stopped and rolled down the window.

"There are plenty of spaces back there," he said, pointing. "You'll see Ginger's van."

"Thanks," she said. She spotted the van, sitting higher than the cars. Ginger and the boys got out and reached them by the time Brooke and Ben had exited the car. She was glad Ginger had told her to wear a sweater. The early morning air was chilly. Ben and the boys didn't seem to notice.

When Jake walked up to them, Brooke figured Ginger must have stationed him at the parking lot entrance.

Ginger and Jake had flashlights, as did many others. They made their way from the parking lot, around the church, and past two rows of homes and to the beach.

While holding Ben's hand, Brooke saw people walking from all directions, many using flashlights to light their paths as they stumbled through the darkness, making their way toward the great rustic wooden cross, stark and black against a deep gray background where the sky could not be distinguished from the ocean.

Ushers were stationed along the beach to hand out programs. The people kept coming. Voices were subdued as they came onto the beach. A hush settled over the crowd as, one by one, the lights flicked off. Everyone stood together on uneven, soft beach sand. The only sound was that of the power of an ocean that could hardly be seen in the darkness. Hundreds of people, like dark silhouettes, stood beneath the cross.

How many had seen Jesus die on the cross? Brooke contemplated. *His mother? A few disciples? Several curious onlookers? Roman soldiers? Had their hopes died when Jesus died on that cross? Does Jesus know that's how I have felt? Like my feet are not on solid ground? That the light that shines on my life's path is as unnatural and single-beamed as a flashlight? Why are all these people here? Are they curiosity seekers? Are they worshipers? But more important, why am I here? To teach a religious holiday to Ben? Or—*

The gasp of hundreds of people stopped her thoughts. Brooke too, gasped. Even Ben, knowing something spectacular was occurring, looked up at her and pointed ahead. Brooke nodded. Yes, she saw it. A golden arc of light appeared far off in the distance and seemed to rise from the ocean, as if God were separating the heavens from the water.

One voice began, then others joined in. Never had Brooke seen or heard anything so spectacular. Human voices raised in praise to the Lord as He painted a masterpiece across the sky before their very eyes. "God sent His Son," they sang while the great golden sphere dispelled the darkness, began turning the sky pink, gold, and blue. The rays glinted against the cross and cast a golden glow on the faces of those emerging from the darkness into the light.

"Because he lives, I can face tomorrow," the words rang out, stronger and stronger as light illuminated the programs. Brooke could see the words on the program. But more important, she could feel the words.

When the group, most with their hands lifted toward heaven, sang with assurance about Jesus being a risen Savior and the words rang out, "Christ Jesus lives today. He walks with me and talks with me, along life's narrow way," Brooke saw how the sun made a pathway from the heavens, so far away the distance was unimaginable. And yet, it was right here for her to see. The rays reached across miles and miles of mighty ocean waves, making a golden, glistening pathway from the sun to the shore.

How narrow was the beam of the flashlights. Even if everyone there put their beams together, that would be as nothing compared to the light that God was bestowing on the people gathered at the cross.

Brooke's throat was too closed to sing, but the words were like a balm to her soul as they sang that Jesus is the hope of all who seek Him and the help of all who find Him.

"I was blind, but now I see," reverberated even more strongly than the sound of the mighty ocean. *Does this crowd of Christians, when bonded together in one accord, have as much power as that of the ocean?*

The preacher spoke a few words about living by faith, based on Romans 1:17. *Can I do it?* Brooke wondered. *I believe in You, Jesus. I've believed in You since I was a little girl. But how much faith do I have? Can I. . .live by faith?*

Light, almost blinding in its brightness against a blue sky shown down upon them as the group broke up while singing about facing tomorrow, "because He lives."

Have I been stumbling around in the dark with a flashlight? Brooke wondered as they made their way back toward the church in the natural light of God's creation. She glanced at Ginger, who smiled through her tears. Brooke realized her own face was wet. A glance at Jake revealed a swipe of his hand across his cheek.

"Stay for breakfast," Ginger entreated when they reached the church.

"Yeah, let's do," Ben pled.

Brooke had thought they'd go home after the sunrise service, but now she didn't want to lose this wonderful feeling of peace and assurance that she hadn't felt in so many years. She wanted to be with this group of believers—and with God.

Breakfast in the fellowship hall turned out to be a feast of colored eggs, sausage and egg casserole, ham croissants, Danish and other pastries, yogurt, juice, and coffee. For so long, Brooke had wondered how it would feel to go to a singles' class after having been married. But on this day, nothing was said about why a person was single. There were so many visitors there wasn't time for more than introductions and each person telling where they were from—if they lived on Hilton Head or were visiting.

Jessica Lawler came over to speak to Brooke, introduce her husband, and ask how things were going. Brooke was able to mean it when she thanked the realtor for sending Jake Randolph her way.

Brooke remembered asking Ginger if God had sent her. She'd said it rather jokingly, but now she wondered if it were true. Her vision of walking into a sanctuary in a strange place had been unfounded. By the time of the worship service, she'd been introduced to so many people and had smiled so much that she felt like she belonged. It helped too, sitting on the pew next to Ginger with Ben on the other side of her. Jake sat at the other end of the pew next to Mike.

When they first sat down, Brooke was aware of the long double rows of pews, the color of light oak, separated by a wide strip of royal blue carpet reaching to the steps of the raised dais on which stood a wide lectern with white Easter lilies all across the front. Great exposed wooden beams, like dark oak, slanted high, crossing in the center, forming a cathedral ceiling. Recessed lights shone from between each beam. Behind the dais, partitioned off by a low wooden railing, sat gold velvet chairs. Above the choir loft was a round, stained-glass window of multi-colored Christian symbols such as the lamb, the dove, and the cross.

Brooke forgot about the lovely interior as soon as the choir members in white robes filed in and began to sing "Christ the Lord Is Risen Today." When the choir presented their message in song, Brooke could feel the words, "Awake my soul, and sing," and when the congregation sang, she joined in.

"We're going to my parents' house for traditional Easter dinner," Ginger said. "Come eat with us."

When Brooke began to shake her head, Ginger tempted, "Ham, melt-in-your-mouth sweet potatoes with marshmallows on top, little green peas—"

"No, really, we need to get home."

After a long look, Ginger nodded and smiled. "I understand. I'll call you soon," she said and squeezed Brooke's arm affectionately.

Brooke had the feeling that Ginger really did know how she felt. Ginger too was a single mom who'd no doubt had all the same feelings Brooke was having—wanting to trust God and people, wondering how things were going to work out and if she should accept offers of kindness, wondering if it were kindness or pity?

When she arrived home, Brooke remembered that there had been a quick rain shower on Saturday, but her house was dry. Her eyes focused on the corner of the house.

I wonder, she thought, *can the corners of my life be fixed? Can I face tomorrow with faith, and hope?*

❧

When tomorrow came, Brooke began the day with a prayer.

Then before breakfast she read a Bible verse to Ben and they prayed together. After she had him help clear the table and make his bed, he went out to play with Taz, and she set about getting rid of the grime still in most of the house. It had been good to spend Sunday as a day of worship and rest.

During the week, she tackled the house with renewed vigor, feeling more at peace with herself, her situation, the friendship that was developing with Ginger, Ben's friendship with a boy his own age, and even her changing feelings about Jake Randolph. She hadn't felt like contacting him yet about other repairs, but when Friday's forecast said rain might be expected on the weekend, she called Ginger and asked if she thought Jake could check out her roof. The dark stains on the once-white kitchen ceiling looked rather ominous.

Right after she hung up the phone, she heard a knock on the door, and her immediate thought was that Jake Randolph had ESP and had decided to come and see what she needed. However, when she answered the door, there stood Ben's Sunday school teacher, whom Brooke had met but whose name she didn't remember.

"Hi," said the petite brunette, about her own age, dressed in a pretty summer dress. "I'm Evelyn," she said. "Ben was in my class Sunday."

"Come in," Brooke said, after warning her about the precariously hanging screen door. She was grateful that several weeks of airing out the place had eliminated the mildew odor. The living room was cleaned, although spots were visible on the carpet and watermarks were on the upholstery on the couch and easy chair.

"I don't have everything fixed up yet," she apologized, "but everything's been cleaned, although the spots didn't come out."

"At least you have furniture," Evelyn replied, "which is more than I can say about myself. I'm a single mom too and live with my parents. That's about to change, though." She promptly sat on the big stain in the easy chair. "Is Ben here?"

Ben and Taz chose that moment to enter the room.

"Uh uh," Brooke chastened, just as Ben got that knowing look on his face and said, "Taz, go home." The dog ran.

Brooke grinned as she sat on the couch. "The dog knows he's going to get a cookie. Well, a dog biscuit, but we call it a cookie."

Soon, Ben returned, and when Evelyn said, "Hello, Ben," he stuck out his hand. Before Brooke could ask if his hands were clean, Evelyn shook his hand. *Oh, well,* Brooke remembered. *She has a child too.*

"I have a little something for you, Ben," Evelyn said and held out a small white bag.

"Oh, neat. Look, Mom," he said and pulled out a book and handed it to Brooke.

"Oops," she said, as a gold bookmark decorated with a big red apple fell out. She returned it to the book and read the title. "*Apples from God,*" she said. "How nice."

"Thank yooooou!" Ben said to Evelyn, and then began to pull red apples from the bag.

"He loves books," Brooke said and then laughed lightly. "And apples too."

Evelyn smiled. "We give a bag of apples and a copy of that book to all the children in the area who visit our class."

"Can I go out and read it in the swing?" Ben asked. Brooke nodded her permission.

Evelyn gave a rundown of activities for children in the church, saying that Ben fit right in on Sunday and listened eagerly to the stories.

Brooke nodded. She knew Ben was an outgoing boy. And it was certainly her responsibility to channel his energy in the right direction. "He has a friend there already," Brooke noted. "Danny Harris."

"Yes," Evelyn said. "I saw you sitting in the sanctuary with Jake and Ginger."

She thought I was sitting with Jake? "Ginger's been a lifesaver to me."

Evelyn nodded. "She's a wonderful example to all us single moms," she said with feeling, then stood. "Speaking of being a mom, I need to get home. My mom keeps Sara all day and cooks supper for me, so I'd better scoot."

Brooke stood too and thanked her for the visit and the gift to Ben.

"Hope to see you Sunday, Ben," Evelyn said as she left and waved good-bye to Brooke.

"And the apple fell out of the tree on the boy's head and it had a worm in it," Ben said as if he were reading.

"What? The boy's head had a worm in it?" Brooke shrieked, and Ben laughed while kicking his feet out in glee. Brooke sat carefully on the swing with its still-rusty chain and grabbed the book. "Why, you little kidder," she said playfully. "You just said that to get me to read it to you, didn't you?"

"Yup," he replied, his big dark eyes shining, melting her heart. *Oh,* she thought, *I must not fail to train up this precious boy in the right way.*

nine

Jake came on Saturday, although the forecast was showers. Beneath the graying sky, he was nailing away on the roof at lunch time. Brooke didn't like the idea of leaving someone at her house working while she went away, but she had an afternoon appointment to take Taz to get his rabies shot. After she and Ben ate, she thought perhaps Jake had made a special effort to work for her on Saturday, so she made him a sandwich and took it out to the swing.

She walked out into the yard until she could see him on the roof. She did not want to give the impression that just because she was a friend of Ginger's that automatically she expected Jake to be her friend. However, she could at least treat him like she would any other ordinary human being—or the dog.

Why am I having such difficulty relating to this man? she asked herself. She didn't have time to stand around and try to find an answer at the moment. Perhaps it was because he seemed always on the fringes of her activity but they'd never even had a decent conversation.

"Mr. Randolph," she called, "we have to take Taz to the vet. There's a sandwich on the swing if you want it."

He lifted his hand in a kind of salute. "Thank you, ma'am," he said. " 'Preciate that."

She felt a drop of rain. "It's raining. You might be gone when we get back. Just send an invoice." She remembered his talking about free work, which she didn't want, and quickly added, "And for the corner."

"Yes, ma'am," he said, and she could feel his broad smile, reminding her of what a ruggedly handsome man he was. More than that, she couldn't imagine a more appealing sight than a strong, muscular man like him with tears in his eyes at the foot of a rugged cross. Shaking away that image and annoyed with herself for her thoughts, she quickly turned and hurried Ben and Taz into the back seat of the car. The last thing she needed was to be thinking of a man! *But,* she reminded herself, as if she needed to be defended, *my thoughts about him were mainly spiritual!*

❧

Mr. Randolph! Jake thought with a shake of his head, watching Brooke Haddon and her son drive away. She wouldn't call him Jake, making sure he knew to keep his distance. He could accept that. He could understand it. Once your life had been turned upside down, you could never quite have that innocent kind of trust that once was a part of you.

At the same time, part of him wished he could be that happy-go-lucky kind of guy he used to be and let a girl know he was interested in her right away. In his college days he could do that, and when he'd been rejected a couple of times, he'd just shrugged it away. After all, there were plenty of others, eager to accept his advances.

He wasn't like that anymore. His approach to life wasn't the same as in his younger days. He'd learned the hard way that you couldn't always take a person at face value or at their word.

Maybe after today, Brooke Haddon would realize he was not a scam artist or a lecher—just a hard-working man doing his job, and yes. . .hoping to favorably impress her.

He hadn't met a woman in years that sparked this kind of

interest in him. Maybe it had started because she didn't trust him and he wanted to correct that impression. Maybe it was because of her physical attractiveness that a seeing man couldn't deny. But a lot of it had to do with watching her trying to get back into the mainstream of life after a devastating personal experience and beginning her efforts at a church service.

He knew how hard it was to face people when inside you felt like a tidal wave had come along and swept away everything in life that you'd thought was important.

He would never forget the day two average-looking men in business suits got out of a car in front of his shop when he opened it up.

"Jake Randolph?" one asked.

"Yes, what can I do for you?" Jake asked with a smile. He had a lot to smile about that morning. He was working on the biggest job he'd had since he and Martin Gage bought the business from Jake's dad after his heart attack. Yep, business was booming, Jake was saving money, he and Meagan had spent a night to remember last night and were talking marriage, and the sun was shining. So what was there not to smile about?

"A Martin Gage work with you?" the talking man asked.

"We're partners," Jake said. These men definitely looked like customers. Maybe wanted a mall or business offices built. "Come on in. Martin should be here any minute now."

Jake led them to the office, offered them chairs, made a pot of coffee while they asked usual questions that prospective clients might ask. When the coffee was done, they refused a cup. When Martin came in and was introduced, they flashed badges, read them their Miranda rights, and said they were under arrest.

"Arrest?" Jake stammered, looking from the men to Martin, whose face had turned red as a tomato.

"For refusing to pay income taxes for the past two years," the man explained.

"Give me the bill. I'll pay them," Jake said.

"Doesn't work that way," the man said bluntly. "You were given warnings and plenty of time. Let's go for a little ride."

On that ride, when Jake looked at Martin, his partner turned his head and looked the other way. Without a word from him, it was plain as day what had happened.

Martin had worked for Jake's dad for many years. After a beam fell on Martin's leg, Jake's dad brought him in as office assistant while he recuperated. After his leg healed, Martin knew his leg would never be the same and realized was getting a little age on him, so he asked to stay on as assistant bookkeeper. He'd always been a good worker, so Jake's dad had no problem with that.

And Jake had no problem with Martin's interest in gambling. After all, Jake wasn't exactly lily-white, so who was he to spout off about it? It was Martin's business what he did with his own money. After Jake's dad decided to sell the business, Martin's big win during a trip to Vegas enabled him to come in as a partner.

That suited Jake. He liked Martin. He'd been a good employee for Randolph Construction on both outside and inside jobs. Never in a million years did he suspect Martin would be guilty of this kind of "inside job." After all, who would suspect a man would steal from his own company or not pay income tax on his own business? *Unless,* the thought hit hard, *he'd had a lot of gambling losses!*

Jake expected this would all be over in a short while. His one phone call was to his dad's attorney, who came down, and after Jake posted his own bail bond, he was free to go until he was to appear for trial.

He went immediately to Meagan. The moment he said, "I've been arrested for income tax evasion," her mouth dropped open and she looked like someone had turned her to stone.

"I didn't do it, Meagan. It's Martin. He ran the office. He kept the books. And now, he's gambled away his part of the profits and didn't pay the taxes. That's why he's been saying things like wanting to get back down to Vegas where the big bucks are. But I didn't suspect he'd do something like this."

"You're part owner, Jake," she said as if he thought her a fool for believing he hadn't known what was happening. "And you told me about all that money you've been saving." She threw up her hands. "Oh, Jake! How could you?"

That was the second shock wave of the day, and only the beginning of the personal earthquake that hit on the day of the trial. Martin had plea-bargained, pled guilty, was put on probation, and was out walking the streets.

Against the advice of the attorney, Jake refused to plead guilty to something he didn't do. Surely the jury would understand that he had principles, morals. After all, Martin had said he was guilty. But the jury adhered to what the law had to say. Jake was a partner. Ignorance was no excuse. Jake was guilty.

"Six months in federal prison!" the judge sentenced, and at the pound of the gavel, Jake felt like he'd fallen through a crack in the ground and the earth had swallowed him up.

A flash of lightning brought Jake to the realization he was not still in prison. He was on probation and on top of Brooke Haddon's roof with a hammer in his hand and raindrops falling on his head. He'd make a perfect lightning rod! With that thought he climbed down, gulped his sandwich, and did one more little chore before packing up his tools and feeling quite good about the jobs he'd done for Brooke Haddon.

Surely, she would be. . .at least. . .cordially appreciative.

❧

When Brooke and Ben returned, a steady rain was falling. Since Taz wasn't supposed to go beyond the kitchen, Ben ran around the house toward the back yard, with Taz racing beside him. Brooke's eyes rose to the roof, but Jake wasn't there. She sat and looked at the house a moment longer. Jake apparently did good work. The new wood needed to be painted, but then, so did the whole cottage. She sighed. The main thing was to keep the rain and the bugs out.

With that thought, she jumped out of the car and headed for the house. When she reached the porch, she saw a folded paper plate underneath the screen. Couldn't he have taken it out back to the trash can?

Oh, well! She carefully opened the screen door and gasped. It stayed in place. It was fixed. He'd put on a new hinge. Well, how nice! Or, was it? Depended upon how much it cost.

She reached down and picked up the paper plate. It was folded, and he'd written what looked like an invoice:

Roof—not finished
The corner—my "freebie"
Screen hinge—$3.98
4 screws— .20
_____
Total due————$4.18

Was that man trying to get her attention? Well, maybe she didn't have much money and didn't know how to make repairs herself, but this was ridiculous. She didn't have to accept charity. It wasn't as if she were totally broke, it's just that the supply of money wasn't limitless and she wanted to stay with Ben this summer before he started to school.

And, Brooke thought in consternation, *no matter how charming or appealing Jake might be, I do not want to feel beholden to any man.*

Not wanting to think about Jake and how she should handle the invoice, she simply tossed the paper plate on top of the refrigerator and tried to forget it. She would go about her business and deal with that when her mind was clearer. In the meantime, she would simply wait and see if Jake Randolph tried to press her with coming around to do other repairs.

He didn't, and she told herself she was glad. Ginger didn't even mention him when she called mid-week and encouraged Brooke to take advantage of the church's "Mother's Day Out" program. Brooke said she'd take a look and see Ben's reaction.

"Cool!" he said when he saw the fenced-in children's playground, complete with sand, tunnels, slides, monkey bars, swings, and about anything a little child's active heart could desire.

She assumed "cool" was as good as "neat" when he asked, "Can I stay, Mom?" Danny's eyes also pleaded with her.

"Okay," she said, seeing there were plenty of volunteers to watch them, some of whom she had seen or met on Sunday. And Ginger's boys would be there with him.

Brooke and Ginger spent the morning shopping. Brooke was grateful Ginger knew where to get all the bargains, not only on groceries but on cleaning supplies and household items, including a sale on sheets and towels.

When they returned, Ginger showed Brooke the sunken

prayer garden, a lovely spot between two buildings, surrounded by lush foliage, tall palmettos, and live oaks. She walked down the steps and onto the bricks. She could see how this place was conducive to prayer, as if she had stepped away from life for a moment into a private place to reverently commune with God.

ten

For the first time in years, Brooke felt as eager as Ben to return to church the next Sunday. It was as if her soul were starved for the Bread of Life, which was Jesus.

There were fewer people in the singles' class, and they spent a brief time getting to know each other and introducing those who hadn't met. But most of the class was spent on Bible study since the group met twice a week to interact and talk about personal needs. Brooke liked the class members, the teacher, and the warm friendly feeling of everyone. Jake's friendly manner was the same with everyone, and he usually sat near other guys and they all listened attentively and discussed the Bible passages.

Even the sermon on Sunday morning seemed designed just for her. The pastor read from Romans 8:39 about nothing being able to separate a person from the love of God. "Death can't, life can't, the angels can't, and the demons can't," the man read. A feeling of hope and joy touched Brooke's heart when he read that our fears for today, our worries about tomorrow, and even the powers of hell could not keep God's love away.

Brooke felt both elation and guilt. *Even though my faith isn't strong*, she thought, *God hasn't abandoned me. Ben and I have our needs met, and we have each other. He even brought friends to our door, and this church is filled with caring Christians and people who understand what it's like to be broken and need help beyond what we can give ourselves.*

The song leader stood and asked them to sing "Leaning on the Everlasting Arms."

"What a joy divine. . .what a peace is mine," the people sang, and Brooke was vaguely aware of Ben and Danny rocking back and forth in time with the music.

The real meaning of the words "everlasting arms" escaped Brooke at the moment. The singing seemed to recede into the background as she gazed out over the congregation. She was reminded of how Bruce had said she looked good on his arm. He'd been happy with her until she got pregnant. Then he thought she no longer looked good on his arm. Their son was a burden to him that he hadn't been ready for.

The strands of the hymn kept tugging at her heart and mind. How she'd prayed during those six years of marriage. But the relationship had gone steadily downhill. The prayers weren't answered. She glanced toward the high beams as if to ask if there was really a caring God and if so, where was He during that time.

She quickly looked down again. She mustn't do that. She'd always known there was a God. It was just that she hadn't called upon Him until her marriage had deteriorated beyond repair. And Bruce hadn't seemed to consider God very much.

Now, as if God were speaking to her, Brooke was reminded that God had given her parents who took her in. He'd kept that little cottage tucked away on this resort island for a roof over their heads. He'd given her a wonderful son. Ben had new playmates, and she had a friend she could confide in.

Her glance inadvertently wandered over to her left, and she glimpsed Jake Randolph, whose voice and face were lifted in praise to the Lord. Despite her aversion to receiving his charity, she could even be grateful that God had sent her a much-needed handy-man.

"Come eat lunch with us," Ginger said, after the service ended and they were all in the parking lot. "We're having every boy's favorite."

"Pizza!" Mike shouted, and the others followed with, "Yea! Yea!"

Ginger took a deep breath and blew out through her lips as she shook her head of auburn curls and glanced at Brooke with chagrin. "We can't afford pizza for you guys with bottomless stomachs. We're having every boy's second favorite meal, cooked on the grill." She looked at Mike. "Got a clue?"

"Yeah. Barbecue chicken." He grinned mischievously while his mother said, "You know better."

He nodded. "Grilled bread! And water to drink."

"That's exactly what you deserve," said a male voice. Jake had walked up and rested his hands on Mike's shoulders. Mike looked up at Jake with admiration in his eyes.

Brooke wondered how she could graciously get out of this. She could use a friend, but not a male one. Additional complications she'd didn't need! She was about to say she still had a house to get in shape, but Danny interrupted with a plea to his mother. "Can Ben come, Mom? And bring his puppy?"

"Yeah, yeah," the other boys chimed in, and Ben tugged on the skirt of her dress. "Oh, Mom. You should've seen how 'cited Taz was when they was at our house. He was jumping all over creation. Can we go?"

They all laughed at his childish prattle, and how "'cited" he was over the prospect of playing with his new friends. Brooke recognized the expression of doing something "all over creation" as one her mom had inadvertently passed down to her. Now Ben was saying it. Like mother, like child?

Just as she opened her mouth to refuse, Jake spoke. "I could keep an eye on these guys for awhile and give you two a chance to get acquainted." He tousled the hair of George, who'd moved closer to him.

There was really no reason to refuse. To do so might look suspicious, as if she had started thinking about Jake as something other than a repairman. Anyway, she needed to talk to him about that carpentry bill.

"Okay, thanks," Brooke said to Ginger, avoiding looking at Jake. "But Taz?" she began.

"Oh, go get him," Ginger encouraged. "Mike can go with you and give directions to our house. It's only a couple of miles from you and easy to find. You might want to bring a bathing suit too. We have a pool."

"Bring a little dog food with you," Jake said.

For an instant, Brooke wondered if he were testing her to see if she was feeding the dog people-food. On second thought, he probably was just thinking of the puppy—as if she didn't have sense enough to know his feeding time.

George and Danny wanted to go too, and Brooke assured Ginger that would be fine. It might take four boys to hold onto a dog so " 'cited" he jumped all over creation.

Brooke exchanged her dress for jeans but didn't bother with a bathing suit because she had no intention of running around half-dressed in front of Jake. Ben changed into play clothes. He moaned that he didn't have bathing trunks.

"I have two," Danny said. "You can wear one of mine."

Mike shrugged. "You can swim in your clothes if you want to."

Just in case, Brooke picked up an extra set of play clothes for Ben.

The boys stuffed the box full of puppy on the floorboard of

the back seat. That was useless! Before she could pull out of the driveway, the boys had the puppy literally climbing all over them and the car.

In spite of puppy licks and wagging tail in his face as his brother held Taz up to him, Mike was able to give simple and concise directions. "Up this street, turn there, down that road, up that street." After she'd driven about two miles, he exclaimed, "There it is!"

Brooke recognized the low country style house as one that had appealed to her years before. She'd seen many of those, typical of the southern spacious houses that seemed ideal for large families. Steps leading to the front door separated the expansive porch that stretched the entire width of the house. The light brown banister and shutters complemented the cream-colored house which was topped by a gray roof that blended with moss-covered oaks that seemed to offer a protective covering over the house.

A hedge of blooming azaleas—red, coral, and white—adorned the front of the house on each side of the steps and reached around the house. An immaculate green lawn lay like a lush carpet.

"They'll be out back," Mike said after Brooke parked on the white sand and shell driveway at the side of the house, facing a high, light-brown wooden fence. The boys ran yelling to the back of the house by the time Brooke got the box and puppy food out of the car.

Brooke walked through the gate, left open by the boys, closed it behind her, fastened the latch, and walked around the corner of the house when she heard Ginger calling for the boys to come inside and change clothes.

"Leave the puppy out here," Brooke said, glad she'd brought the box. Ben put the puppy down, and it started to run along behind him but couldn't make it up the step. She set the box down, placed the puppy food beside the steps, scooped the puppy up, and put him in the box. His whimpering and scrambling to get out showed his displeasure.

Brooke glanced around at the back yard, understanding why the front of the house seemed to belie that three active boys lived here. The back yard was perfect as a children's playground and looked like a safe haven. The rectangular pool and surrounding concrete took up almost the entire left side of the yard. At the far end of the yard stood a swing set, on white sand, enclosed by timbers. It appeared to be any child's dream with its three swings, a long slide, and a climbing rope beside a ladder leading to a small enclosed landing. Several flowering azalea bushes lent spectacular color, and a yellow jessamine trailed up one corner and along the top of the wooden fence.

The lounge chairs and two chaises, scattered along the pool side, looked particularly inviting. Behind those on the right sat a long picnic table with attached benches. Nearer the open narrow porch on a cobbled area sat a large grill with a domed lid.

Smiling at the perfect picture, Brooke startled out of her reverie, hearing Ginger yell, "Don't get in the pool yet," at the same time the screen door was flung open and four boys dashed across the porch and raced to the swing set. Mike got there first, but let the other three boys take the swings.

"Look, Mom," Ben called. "I'm swinging up to heaven."

"I see," she said, smiling. It hadn't been too long ago that he'd learned how to push himself with his body and feet. He watched his new friend, Danny, and tried to go as high as the other five-year-old boy.

"I know you're out there somewhere, Brooke," Ginger

called from a window. "Come in and make yourself useful."

Just as she turned, ready to step up onto the porch, Jake opened the screen door and stepped out. He greeted her with a nice smile and immediately turned his attention to the dog. "Okay to let Taz out?"

"Sure," she said and clamped her lips shut to keep from telling him not to let Taz fall into the pool. After closing the screen, one backward glance revealed Jake standing with his hands on his hips, chuckling, while the little puppy waddled as fast as he could toward the exuberant boys.

❧

Jake asked himself what he'd expected of Brooke Haddon. Had he thought she'd turn cartwheels just because he repaired her corner and fixed her screen? He needed to keep everything in perspective and just hope that a word or glance from her would indicate she accepted him as a friend—or at least as a human being.

Ginger had said Brooke had had an unpleasant experience with an unfaithful husband before he died in an auto crash. He'd like to talk to her, let her know he understood the difficulties of starting over. He'd like to be her friend, and the more he saw of her, he knew he'd like to be more than a friend.

He dared not stare when Brooke and Ginger brought out food and put it on the picnic table. He had to keep his distance, pretend he wasn't interested. He lectured himself on the fact that Brooke Haddon wasn't there to hobnob with him but to engage in a friendship with his sister and allow her son to play with other children.

He knew Ginger had come to terms with her single status. Unlike some of the singles, she wasn't expecting God to bring a man into her life to make it meaningful. Why couldn't he be as accepting? Common sense told him he didn't stand a chance with a woman like Brooke Haddon, who had been married to a politician who gave her everything. She had an air about her of grace and style, something rather foreign to him.

He stabbed the hotdogs, turning them lest they burn, feeling as if a skewer had done such to his heart. Common sense told him to be realistic. And he had been, since Meagan rejected him. But he hadn't expected someone like Brooke Haddon to come on the scene and disturb his carefully controlled emotional life just by being distantly near.

Face facts, he warned himself. *This can get you nothing but heartache. You're not a teenager now, but a grown man. You're a man with a past. If Brooke Haddon distrusts you now, imagine what she would feel if you told her you were an ex-con on probation.* That had proved to be disastrous with Meagan. So, how in the world could he ever say to a woman like Brooke, "Hey, by the way, I've spent time in federal prison"?

≈

The day was gorgeous, sporting a mild temperature, complete with a clear blue sky and a soft gentle breeze.

Brooke could be grateful that in spite of there being two mothers without husbands and four little boys without daddies, there was a good-natured man around to tell them to wash their hands and then to give thanks to God for the food.

They all held hands as Jake bowed his head and prayed. "Thank You, Lord, for the blessings of this day and those who have come to share this food with us. Thank You for the food, and may it nourish our bodies. Guide us, Lord, that we may use our lives in service to You. In Jesus' name we pray, amen."

After lunch and cleanup, Brooke and Ginger, seated in the

rocking chairs on the porch, held glasses of lemonade and watched. Jake showed the boys how to coax Taz to sit and lie down, then reward him.

So that's why he wanted me to bring puppy food! She should not be so quick to think the worst of men, just because Bruce had disappointed her. Brooke was impressed with how Jake played with the boys. He was actually getting Taz to sit and get down on command. He was making a good impression on her.

She remembered that her politician husband had made a good impression too. So good, she married him. He'd gone to church many Sundays, shook hands, and kissed babies— all for votes. But no, she was not going to be fooled by any seemingly exceptionally caring man again.

After a while Jake said it was time to swim.

"I'll take care of the change," Ginger said, rising. "You just sit here and relax."

ॐ

When Jake returned to the yard, in his bathing trunks, and a towel slung over his shoulders, Ginger and the boys were nowhere in sight. Brooke still sat in the rocker on the porch, looking like she was studying the yellow jessamine at the far corner of the yard, as if she didn't see him.

It wasn't easy figuring out how to relate to her. He'd come to understand a little of how women like Ginger and some of the other single moms felt. He'd heard enough stories of men being abusive or unfaithful. He didn't know Brooke's situation, except that her husband had died a year ago and she was very wary of men. . .or at least of him.

He could at least talk about business, but it was Sunday and he didn't do business on Sunday. He could tell her about the singles' group, but he knew Ginger would do that, probably

had already, and Brooke was already coming to the singles'
Sunday school class.

Why was he having such a hard time relating to her? He
wasn't quite as outgoing as Ginger, but he certainly wasn't
shy by any means. Something about this woman caught him
off-guard. He was behaving like some kid with his first crush
on a girl.

Oh, boy!

"Taz," he called, deciding that was the safest route to take.
"Come."

The dog came running and stood in front of him, his tail
shaking wildly. Jake gave him a piece of food, then tossed
his towel onto a chair, stepped to the side of the pool, and
jumped in.

&

Just because Brooke wasn't interested in a man didn't mean
she couldn't appreciate Jake's bronzed, athletic body as he
smoothly swam several laps across the pool, while the boys
were changing. The combination of his work and swimming
apparently kept him in terrific shape. She needed to do something about her own body. Not that she was out of shape, but
she knew the importance of aerobics and toning.

Soon, ahead of Ginger, the boys came running out, Ben in
a pair of Danny's trunks. They jumped, screaming, into the
pool—except Ben.

Brooke jumped up, ready to run toward him as he teetered
on the edge of the pool while the boys encouraged him to
jump, but he was frozen, scared to jump and scared to move
away.

The boys were yelling for him to jump in. Jake immediately realized the dilemma and told the boys to be quiet.
"Come down the steps," Jake encouraged. "I'll hold your

hand. I won't let you go."

Soon, Jake had Ginger's boys swim away from him and Ben while he gave some basic instructions, and before long Ben was holding onto the side, kicking his feet, sticking his head under. Soon, Jake had him bobbing and gave him instructions on how to float.

"My boys are fish," Ginger said, "thanks to Jake."

"I'm afraid Ben's a rock," Brooke retorted. "The weather in Indiana is quite different than here on this mild-climate island. He never swam much and then only in shallow water. He loves water and had a great time in a plastic pool. But he's not comfortable in deep water.

"It's only three feet at this end," Ginger said.

Before long, Ben was a regular little trooper in the shallow end. When he got past the three-feet level, he'd do what Jake instructed and float or hold his breath and swim toward the side or shallow end. The other boys swam across alone or on Jake's shoulder and would dive off, head first.

Ben wouldn't. "I'll do it next time," he promised.

Brooke was impressed. "Your brother's very good with children and dogs," she said.

Ginger nodded. "I was about ready to throw up my hands and quit before Jake moved in with us. I try to keep the boys from disturbing him too much. But most of the time, he's just like a dad to those boys. We'd be in a pickle without him."

They both gazed out at the man being so patient with the little boys and seeming to love every minute of it. Brooke and Ginger laughed as Taz kept going to the edge of the pool, but the minute water splashed on his face, he'd run away.

Brooke's glance returned to Jake. "I take it he's not married," she commented.

"No, he's single," Ginger said and added quickly, giving

Brooke the impression that her next words were a deliberate change of subject, "By the way, I teach water aerobics here three mornings a week from ten to eleven. There's usually about eight or ten of us. Come join us. Give you a chance to meet some other people."

That sounded wonderful to Brooke. "You're a mind reader. I was thinking about getting into some kind of regular exercise routine. But first, I have to get that house fixed up."

"Um, how long did you say it's been that way?" Ginger asked with a sly grin.

Brooke laughed. "I get your point. And I know with a boy and dog around it's never going to be ship-shape. But I have to try."

Ginger wagged her finger. "All work and no play, you know."

"Okay," Brooke conceded. "Maybe you win. How much do you charge for lessons?"

"Three dollars a lesson or thirty dollars a month, whichever way you want to do it. And you can come once a week or three times a week. A couple of the single moms bring their kids. I know they'd love it if you brought Ben and Taz."

"I just might," Brooke replied, knowing it would be good for both her and Ben. She could manage the cost. "Oh, speaking of money," she said. "I need to talk to Jake about the bill for that corner. He didn't charge me for the repairs. He wrote down that it was free." She spoke somewhat apologetically, knowing she was talking to Ginger about her own brother. "Now, I could understand if the door hinge was free." She shook her head. "But not the corner of the house."

"I know exactly how you feel, Brooke," Ginger said immediately. "You think there are ulterior motives and Jake's going to make a move on you. But it's not just you. Jake does this on every job he takes. Believe me, Brooke, this isn't personal."

Well, Ginger made it pretty clear that Jake wasn't personally interested in her. But you'd think a man like him would be interested in someone! He was good-looking, had a business, was in his mid-thirties, had a great personality, was a Christian and a father-figure to little boys, a good dog-trainer, and a skilled corner-builder. Why, she mused, was this seemingly-extraordinary man living with his sister, and not married, and not with some special woman on this fine Sunday afternoon?

eleven

Mid-morning on Monday, Jake's beeper went off. He kept his beeper on his jeans's belt-loop around his waist and the cell phone in his truck. He finished nailing the last beam in place on the house he and his crew were building, then called his answering service, who filtered his calls and let him know which ones needed immediate attention.

"A Mrs. Haddon sounded anxious to talk with you," the answering service person said.

Jake smiled at the message. Perhaps Ginger, or his job on the corner of the house, had impressed Brooke Haddon well enough for her to decide she could use his services. Yesterday, although he glimpsed her speculative gaze upon occasion, she hadn't seemed offended by him. Maybe today she'd even smile.

He was eager to have this fresh start with her after having gotten off on the wrong foot. However, unless it was an emergency, he never left his crew to finish up for the day. His regular crew all had families, and Jake wanted them to be able to get home for supper with them. At quitting time, Jake and his crew cleaned up around the property, put their equipment into their trucks, and headed for the shop.

Jake washed up while the crew dropped off their equipment. He changed shirts and ran a comb through his hair and then called Ginger to say he wouldn't be there for supper. She said she'd save him something.

Ginger had given him a standing invitation to have supper

with them, and as much as he enjoyed that, he didn't feel obligated. After all, he was only an uncle to Ginger's boys— not their dad, although he felt a deep responsibility to be the kind of Christian example and male influence they needed.

A keen sense of anticipation swept over Jake as he drove along the road headed for the island of Hilton Head. He rode with the windows down. The wind cooled his face and blew his hair and rippled along his arm resting on the window ledge of the car door.

Jake thought of Brooke Haddon's cool gray gaze that morning he'd stopped by when she'd treated him like he was a potential hazard. Then he remembered how the color of her eyes had changed to gray-green when she'd looked up at him with his head hanging over the roof. The expression then had been possible repentance, thanks to the fact he had a sister who'd come to his rescue. Then she'd looked down, and he'd noticed how her long brown lashes had covered her eyes, lying gently above her fair, smooth skin.

Yesterday, while he was proving to be a friend to children and animals, she'd remained cordial. What would it be like this time? Maybe a spring-green look of acceptance? Did she look forward to seeing him again. *Jake! Jake!* he warned himself. *You can't do this. You cannot be interested in any woman until you're off probation, until you've fulfilled the sentence of the court. Only then will you legally have paid your debt to society. So why are you letting your emotions get in a dither?*

He shook his head as if to clear it. Of course, he knew why. He was lonely. He was a thirty-five-year-old single man, with parents he could see any time, working with a crew of spirited guys, involved in the church and particularly with singles, and living in a house where he had access to a sister and three lively boys. His life was full.

But he was lonely.

His parents had each other. His crew had their own lives. Ginger and the boys were not his family.

And you know perfectly well, Jake Randolph, he reminded himself, *there's nothing in the world you can do to change this situation. You're going to Mrs. Haddon's cottage on business. You're a man with a past. A man with a secret. God has blessed you beyond measure. You have to learn to be content with where you are and with what you have—lonely or not.*

He needn't have worried. Brooke met him on the porch, holding onto the screen door he had repaired. Serene gray eyes erased his friendly smile and turned his expression to frustration. He glanced at the corner. Had it fallen in or something? The screen door appeared intact. Her lips formed a firm line.

"Mr. Randolph," she began, holding his paper-plate invoice. "I didn't want to say anything yesterday in front of everybody, but this is ridiculous."

He relented, realizing he'd goofed again. "You're right," he agreed. "I should not have written an invoice on a paper plate. That was totally unprofessional." He sighed, mentally kicking himself in the seat of his jeans with his heavy work boots. How could he have thought that was acceptable? He'd never done such a thing before. The reason was, she'd been so concerned about getting estimates, he'd felt upbeat that his price would beat anybody's around. He wanted to impress her with that. And he wouldn't care if she didn't pay the fee of less than five dollars he'd charged. In a way, that part was a joke. The whole thing was free. But. . .it was unprofessional, and she was letting him know that.

Suddenly it dawned upon him that the reason she had called was not out of any kind of appreciation or to ask him to do further work but to complain about his lack of professionalism. That suddenly nagging fear welled up in him. If any complaint, no matter how minor, got back to the Better Business Bureau, he was sunk. That could be all it would take—one dissatisfied customer.

Jake spoke seriously. "Mrs. Haddon, I'm sorry. Believe me, I would send a legitimate receipt upon payment. I'll run to the shop and draw up a proper invoice if you like." He turned to go.

"Mr. Randolph!" she called, causing him to stop and look back at her over his shoulder. "I'm not referring to the paper plate. I wouldn't care if you wrote it on the side of the house. I'm referring to the amount."

His brows drew together. "You're complaining about the price?"

They stared at each other, both silent, as if he were speaking Chinese and she could only understand Portuguese.

Finally, Jake broke the confusing silence. "You don't need to pay me a cent, Mrs. Haddon. That small amount was sort of a joke. I thought it would make you smile. It's part of my free service. Just. . ." He gestured with his hands. "Throw away the invoice. . .um. . .the paper plate."

He grimaced at his own words. How could a businessman have been so unprofessional as to write an invoice on a paper plate? What was wrong with him? Why did he keep making a complete fool of himself? Particularly in front of the one woman he'd met in years that he'd like to favorably impress.

Brooke let the screen door slam behind her, and she held out the plate to him. "Even if you meant this as a nice gesture, it's totally unacceptable."

He didn't attempt to stop her ranting. Strangely, he was concentrated on how the late evening sun glinted in her steely gray eyes. How the color of indignation tinged the cheeks of her fair, flawless skin. How intriguing the way her soft lips moved as she spoke. Her teeth were very white and straight. There was the tiniest little dimple at one corner of her mouth as she spouted her displeasure with him.

"Maybe I've given the impression that I'm destitute and can't pay my bills," he heard in the back of his mind and forced himself to concentrate on her meaning. "Well, that's not the situation. I am not a charity case!"

So that was it! It was all he could do to keep from laughing out loud. She thought he pitied her or something. Not so. He'd done many jobs for those who couldn't pay up front, and they'd worked out a payment plan. One single mom needed a gate built across the entry to her back porch so her toddler would have a safe place to play outside without falling down the steps or wandering off. The job hadn't cost much by his standards, but with her limited income, they'd worked out a plan and she'd paid a few dollars a month, taking over a year to get it paid off.

"It wasn't charity, Mrs. Haddon."

"Just what would you call it then, Mr. Randolph?"

Her eyes dared him to have a satisfactory answer. He understood her now in plain English words and human body language. He knew she suspected he was trying to impress her for some personal reason and she was trying to convey that such attempts would be useless.

"I've given the wrong impression from the moment we met," he said, glancing toward the graying sky as if seeking help from beyond. He looked back at her then, his face serious. "It's my water-basin theory, Mrs. Haddon," he said. "If you have a few minutes, I'd like to explain it to you."

He felt her skepticism as she stared. "Water basin?" she

queried, looking at him as if they'd reverted to speaking in foreign languages.

This kind of problem had never occurred before. He'd always done his work, added a free job, explained why he did a free job, and it had been accepted and appreciated. Why was this going so wrong? Maybe he should just write out a new invoice or charge her for the corner and let it go.

But that thought hit hard in his chest. He wanted this woman to believe in him, trust him, even like him. Maybe he'd wanted that too much since that first morning when he'd walked into her back yard and thought there was something unidentifiably intriguing about her. Perhaps it was the mystery of her situation. Perhaps it was her instant wariness of him. Perhaps it was because, watching her, the little boy, and a dog, he felt that deep-seated loneliness, or longing for such a life—a cottage, a woman, a little boy, a dog.

&

Why am I fighting that man? Brooke asked herself. *I know he's in the construction business. His sister, with whom I felt instant camaraderie and want for a friend, vouched for him. His work on the corner is an excellent recommendation. He has not shown any indication of improper behavior.*

Why couldn't she just take him at face value, accept his charitable gesture, regard him as the brother of a woman who offered friendship, and just let it go?

Instead, she had to make an issue of it. She hadn't refused Ginger's food, nor had she questioned it. But a gift from a man was a different thing. She could reciprocate Ginger's hospitality, but Jake was another thing.

It had been failure that set her feet on the right path. After returning to her parents' home, trying to be a good mom to Ben while settling up the bills, then becoming involved in church and depending on the Lord, she felt she had become strong. It had been time to make a move and start a life for herself and Ben without the help of her parents.

She would do it. And she would do it without charity. She'd have to be frugal, but there were definitely others who needed charity more than she. There were always her parents she could fall back on, if necessary. And she knew that if there were a great financial need for Ben, the Haddons would come through. She just didn't want to have to resort to calling upon them.

But was that any reason to be rude to a man offering nothing more than his help and kindness? This was no big deal. All she had to do was tell him in a calm way that she would pay for the repair of that corner, period.

"I need to check on Ben," she said. "He's out back."

"I'll walk around," Jake said, beginning to move as he spoke.

Brooke hurried through the house and reached the back door by the time Jake got there. Ben and Taz were playing tug-o'-war with a sock.

"Hey, Ben. Looks like you and Taz have a battle going there."

"Yeah. And I think I'm about to pull his teeth out."

Jake laughed. "I don't know about that. He'd probably let go before he hurt himself. But if you let him pull on cloth like that, he'll think it's all right to chew on cloth in the house. He wouldn't know the difference between chewing on a sock or chewing on clothes and furniture."

"He likes it," Ben said, looking at the dog pulling as hard he could on the sock, his back legs having trouble keeping his balance as he pulled back. Then Ben let go and Taz began to chew on the sock. Ben looked up at Jake with big soulful eyes. "He liked that bread you told us not to feed him, too. But boy, did he get sick. Didn't he, Mom?" He glanced at Brooke, standing on the porch, watching the exchange. "Mom was up all night cleaning Taz, and the kitchen, and herself, and—"

"Ben," Brooke said, looking away from Jake's knowing glance and small grin. "I think he gets the point. Taz had quite a time of it. From now on, it's dog food."

"An occasional snack's all right," Jake said, "but a steady diet of people food just doesn't sit well with a puppy. Hey, you want to learn to play ball with him?"

Ben's eyes got big. "Yeah."

As much as he would enjoy doing so, Jake remembered he wasn't here to entertain the child or train the dog. Mrs. Haddon had called him here to complain about the bill. "Right now, your mom wants to talk business with me." He turned questioning eyes toward Brooke.

She spread her hands. She understood what he'd said about a dog chewing up things in the house, and she'd known of dogs doing that. She couldn't keep Taz outside until they had some kind of enclosure, and she didn't want to chain him up. She shrugged. It might be good to teach the dog a few tricks. Give Ben a purpose other than pulling on one end of a sock. She relented. "If you want to show him, go ahead."

While Ben rushed inside to get a rubber ball and puppy food, Jake knelt down and gently pinched Taz's nose to make him let go of the sock, which he then threw onto the porch.

After Ben came out, Brooke sat on the top step, with her elbows on her jeaned legs and her jaw resting in the palms of her hands, watching the two do what a father and son might do.

Jake explained to Ben, "The main reward should not be the food, but love. So when he does what you tell him, say, 'Good boy.' " Jake showed Ben how to toss the ball a short way, command the puppy to fetch, then say, "Give it to me," or "Bring it here," or something like that. "Don't throw it a long way until he learns. And don't give him a treat unless he does what you say. Okay?"

"Okay," Ben said, and after watching Jake perform the exercise, he was ready to try.

"Very good," Jake said and mussed Ben's dark curls. Ben looked up at him admiringly.

What a lesson, Brooke thought, remembering all the nice things Bruce had given her when all she'd wanted was love. And little Ben responded with glowing eyes when Jake mussed his hair. Yes, that what the world needed, love, sweet love. Puppy dogs, little boys, and grown women too. She wondered just who loved this interesting man who took time to play with a little boy and a dog.

"You practice," Jake said. "When the puppy tires of it, just stop and let him play the way he wants to. As long as he's not destructive."

While Ben and Taz tirelessly played the game, quite effectively, Jake and Brooke watched and laughed. Sometimes Taz would ignore the ball and Ben would forget and give him a piece of food anyway. "Oops, I forgot," he'd say, and Jake would reply, "That's okay. Try again."

Try again seemed to lodge in Brooke's brain. Maybe that's what she should do with Jake. Not be angry with him because he was a man or for what Bruce did to her.

Brooke could readily see that a dog would be a better pet if he were disciplined, just as children and parents had a better lifestyle with order and discipline. Watching Jake with Ben served to remind Brooke that a little boy needed guidance from a dad. She would make sure Ben's needs were met, but just as her own life would have been lacking without her father, she was aware that Ben's was lacking without a dad to spend time with him. Could Jake be a good male influence for Ben, as Ginger said he was for her boys?

"Keep on until he gets tired of it," Jake said. "I need to talk with your mom."

twelve

Jake walked over to the step and stood at the side, reaching up to hold onto the banister. "Mrs. Haddon. If it would make you feel better to pay for that corner, then I'll take the money. But I would appreciate you hearing me out on that."

"The. . .water-basin thing?" she asked, trying not to appear too skeptical.

"Exactly," he said, appearing quite serious as he walked in front of her and sat beside her on the top step.

With knees spread wide, Jake folded his hands and rested his forearms on his thighs, looking out toward Ben and Taz, but Brooke thought he was looking beyond the boy and dog—even beyond the sky turning to gold and pink.

"There was a time when I lost everything and had no money. I decided to give one hundred percent to my work and offer a free service of some kind so the customers would ask why and I could witness to them, telling them that the reason is because I'm a follower of Jesus Christ, who admonishes us to do good to others, to be charitable. If the person is interested, I witness further. If they're not interested, then I've at least attempted to plant a seed, and they will remember that free gift. Jesus gave freely to us—the gift of eternal life is ours if we just receive it. Just accept it."

What a wonderful attitude, Brooke thought. And yet, she'd treated him like he was beneath contempt. But then, she hadn't known him. And some people knew how to put a spin on anything and make themselves look good. She mustn't be judgmental, but she could look at a person's fruit in order to evaluate his character.

Stealing a glance at Jake, she saw what appeared to be a sincere man, a true Christian who was serious about his commitment to the Lord. His attitude was commendable. "What about. . .the water-basin?" she asked.

He nodded and smiled, the glorious sunset reflecting a spark of gold in his warm brown eyes. "That's what gave me the idea," he said. "Our preacher talked about it one Sunday morning during the worship service. He read the Scripture where Jesus took a wash basin and towel and washed the disciples' feet. Jesus then told His disciples to do the same."

Brooke's head turned toward him. "You belong to a foot-washing group?"

He grinned. "No, but that might be good for a lot of us to do, literally. The example was for us to serve each other. When I do at least one repair job free of charge, the customers ask me why. Then I have the opportunity to tell them that I do it because I'm a Christian. Jesus taught that we should do good to others. We should serve them. This is part of my service."

"That's commendable," Brooke said while a thought pressed in on her mind. If she were going to be interested in a man, ever again, she'd want it to be someone like Jake.

Feeling the blush in her cheeks, she looked down at the toes of her scuffed tennis shoes. "Do others give you such a hard time about it, as I did?"

He laughed. "No, but I don't generally barge in the way I did with you. Most of my customers know my company's reputation and come to me. Jessica, the realtor, lets me know about some clients, and she recommends me to some people before I approach them. She felt your situation was an emergency and that you were planning to stay, with a child, in a house that might not be habitable."

"I'm just not trusting enough," Brooke admitted.

"I understand that," Jake said. "I have the same trouble at times. Ginger and other singles we work with find it difficult after they've lost trust in someone or something."

"It's not always fair to the other person," Brooke said.

He smiled. "I don't think you were unfair to me. Sometimes, the people we trust most disappoint us. It's a fact of life that we need to be aware of and yet try to not let it get in the way of interaction, of friendship."

She nodded, knowing she mustn't let the past control her life. *I want interaction and friendship. But. . .not yet!*

"Well," she said suddenly, looking away from his questioning eyes that seemed to say that he thought she had some kind of answer, when in truth she knew she certainly did not. "Now that I've accepted your explanation, I'll run in and get my money."

She returned with a five-dollar bill. "Keep the change," she said.

He didn't argue. Rather he simply said, "Thank you," and stuck the bill in his pocket. "I'll paint the corner of the house if you'd like."

"Yes, I want that," she said, plopping down beside him again. "I have a lot of fixing up to do around here."

He nodded. "I know there are several roof shingles to be nailed down," he commented.

"That's for sure," she agreed. "And I have a kitchen ceiling with brown splotches all over it, two leaky faucets, broken window panes, a temperamental lock on the front door, missing slats in the front banister, a pitiful picket fence." She paused and shook her head. "That's for starters."

"Obviously, no one has lived in it for awhile," he commented.

"Well, nobody's been here since the hurricane hit. Before that, there were renters. Doesn't look like too much damage, but there are a lot of minor repairs to be done, and the whole house needs painting or wallpaper. Are those the kinds of things you do?"

"I do a little bit of everything," he said. "Me and my crew work a five-day week, and I moonlight on Saturdays. Right now, we're working on a half-million-dollar house on the beach. But we also have jobs like replacing a set of steps. It might be twenty steps leading to an upper deck or it might be two steps on a porch." He smiled. "I'm the owner, but I'm also my own secretary-treasurer, accountant, handy-man, and part of the clean-up crew."

"Wow! Jack of all trades," Brooke said, then caught her breath. She shot him a sideways glance. "I don't mean to imply you're master of none."

He didn't laugh, just looked at her seriously. "I can't do everything. I have men on the crew who are much better than me at certain aspects of building. Tim's the best roofer you could find. Marcia can't always hammer a nail in straight, but she can paint a room without leaving a streak or an air bubble. But that's part of owning a business—employing workers with different skills. I'll tell you this, Mrs. Haddon. I give it my best. I don't scrimp anywhere. I don't get by with cheap materials. I don't put my stamp of approval on a project until I think God would approve. My crew and I have a prayer each morning before we start working. That keeps us where we ought to be."

Maybe I should have a prayer right now, Brooke thought, *to keep my mind where it ought to be. I have no business*

*whatsoever letting a man come into my life and into the life
of my boy and his dog and sit here talking like we're close or
something. So we go to the same church. Big deal! He and
Jessica Lawler go to the same church too. Does that mean
anything personal? Apparently not, since Jessica had been at
church with her husband.*

Forcing herself to look away from the interesting way the
light formed a golden gleam in his warm brown eyes, she
spoke quickly. "I think I should probably finish the roof or
repair the windows."

Jake nodded. "I'll be glad to work up an estimate."

"I would appreciate that," Brooke said.

They sat for a moment in silence, then Jake stood. "If it's
all right with you, I'll go ahead and measure the broken window panes and stop by tomorrow evening after work and
bring you an estimate on those and the roof. Oh, I can paint
the corner too."

Brooke nodded.

"Good night, then," he said and called good-bye to Ben.

"This is a good trick, huh, Jake?"

Brooke knew Ben was playing with a Tonka truck, filling
it with sand, dumping it, making mounds that Taz pawed
through, and then beginning again, but it only now dawned
upon her what Ben was doing. He was hiding dog food in the
mounds, and Taz was finding and eating it.

"It's a good trick if you realize that's his supper. He mustn't
have too much food either. The bag tells you how much he
should get," Jake told him. "Tell you what, if your mom
agrees, when I stop by tomorrow, I'll help you teach Taz how
to heel, so you can take him for walks without his taking you
for walks."

"Neat!" Ben said. "That's okay. Right, Mom?"

"Well, we don't want to take up too much of Mr. Randolph's time."

"I did offer," Jake said, glancing at her with a broad smile.

Brooke returned the smile, then quickly glanced at Ben. "Time to come in and get cleaned up, Ben. I'll start supper."

Jake said good-bye again and disappeared around the house. Brooke suddenly realized she wasn't apprehensive about him anymore.

Only about *herself*.

❧

On the drive home, Jake denounced himself for the mistakes he'd made with Brooke Haddon. No wonder she thought he had ulterior motives. Would an electrician or a telephone repairman sit down beside her on the step? Would a plumber or a painter? He thought not!

Then why in the name of Sam Hill had he done it? He'd never done that with any of his other female customers. He'd always kept a professional distance. But with her, he was going overboard—and sometimes going overboard indicated you just might sink. What had happened to his good sense?

Maybe Ginger could tell him.

After he ate the supper Ginger had kept in the fridge and then microwaved for him, Jake sat on the top step of the back porch while Ginger sat in a rocking chair and the boys played on the swing set. He told his sister he'd seen Brooke Haddon and Ben that evening.

"I'm behaving as if she's my friend, Ginger. I know you two hit it off right away, and it's not that way between me and Mrs. Haddon." He snorted. "See. She hasn't even asked me to call her by her first name. This is a business proposition, and I'm behaving like it's something personal."

"Maybe it's because you want it to be, Jake," she said. "I

mean, Brooke has some emotional problems to deal with, but otherwise, she's a strong woman. She has looks, guts, maternal instinct, and faith in God."

Jake nodded. Brooke had sun-streaked, golden blond hair and eyes that changed with the color of her clothes, or the grass, or the sky. She had soft lips with a little dimple at one corner of her mouth when she smiled. She had a musical laugh and an angelic expression on her face when she looked at her son. He couldn't deny it when Ginger added, "And Jake, you're a man who hasn't met a woman who appealed to you since Meagan."

Jake gave a short laugh. "I wouldn't go that far," he said. "A lot of women appeal to me, but I've known I can't get involved. I can't even tell them the truth about myself. I know we talked about this before. When I told the truth to Meagan, she turned and ran the other way, so to speak. She didn't trust me anymore."

He picked up a stick and poked at the dirt in front of the step. "Brooke mistrusted me from the first time I pulled up in that truck and offered my services."

"That's because her emotions are in a turmoil, Jake. It's been a year since her husband's death, but the memory is still part of her life, just as Leo's will always be a part of ours. That's inescapable. Brooke shared her husband's dream. Then when she got pregnant, he wanted her to choose. She chose the unborn baby. She was no longer his dream girl. They drifted apart. His goal was ambition and power. Hers was family life and her son. Then her husband was unfaithful. Now he's dead. I think it's easier for me to be judgmental about my husband, than for her. It's not considered proper to condemn a dead man."

Jake turned and gazed at his sister. "I didn't know all that."

"Of course not," Ginger replied. "We women who've been trampled by a man have to put on a front of having it all together, as if we don't need a man."

Jake thought he knew his sister. But it seemed he learned new things about her everyday. She was a strong woman—in many ways stronger than he, although she was younger. She'd grown in many ways since Leo had discarded her like an old rag. Her faith in herself had been restored. Her faith in God had grown. And yet she was admitting she would like to have a man in her life—not just an older brother. Of course, she would. He'd just accepted her lifestyle and his—until now.

"She's doing a great job with Ben," he said.

Ginger nodded. "It's not easy, Jake. I'd be lost without you."

"You'd make it," he said, reaching over to pat her arm.

"Not as well without you," she said softly. "So! She's going to let you make repairs."

He grinned. "Seems that way."

"You like her, Jake. Don't deny it."

"Very much," he admitted. "But you know I'm in no position to even think about going beyond friendship with a woman."

"Jake," she said surprised. "You told me the business was going well, and besides buying that property, you're saving and—"

"I'm not talking financially, Ginger. Living here has enabled me to save almost all my profits."

"Ha!" she exclaimed. "Your living here has been a lifesaver for me and the boys, Jake. In more ways than financially."

He laughed lightly. "Don't you think we've complimented each other enough for one day?"

Her shoulder lifted in a light shrug. "Well, I probably don't tell you enough how much I appreciate you."

"Mutual admiration society," he said and grinned, then stared into the distance. His brow furrowed.

"What is it, Jake?"

He sighed heavily. "You know I can't consider anything beyond friendship, Ginger."

"Of course you can, Jake. Someday the right woman will understand—"

He interrupted. "Meagan didn't."

"Meagan wasn't the right woman."

"I know that now," Jake said, "but at the time I thought she was. After all we'd meant to each other, it seems she didn't even know me." *But she did know me*, Jake corrected himself silently. *She knew, and she still didn't believe me.*

"Brooke is not Meagan," Ginger reminded him. "She has a lot more maturity and character than your former fiancée."

"But a lot less trust," he said. "Meagan trusted me at the beginning. Brooke's mistrust of me started the first time I pulled up in front of her house and offered my services."

"You said it went well tonight."

"Yes. But I should have checked out the repairs she wanted done, assessed the needs, and suggested some of my crew or the volunteers from the church. Instead, I offered myself several nights after work and Saturday, as long as needed. I play with her boy. I train her dog. I sit beside her on the back step without invitation. I sit on the church pew with her." He sighed and shook his head like he'd committed the crime of the century.

Ginger smiled behind his back. How she'd love to see her brother get a break. And she thought Brooke would be good for Jake. And vice-versa. She understood them both, the reticence of them both. "You said you're going back every night after work?"

"Yep! I committed myself."

"And she didn't tell you not to come."

He glanced around, then turned back to stare at the holes he'd made in the dirt. "Maybe I did wrong there too. I told her about my water-basin theory—my religious reasons for doing work free. Maybe I was playing on her sympathy. It's a little hard to refuse a person when he says he's doing it for the Lord."

"Oh, quit doubting yourself, Jake. I know your intentions are genuine. She will learn that. And I don't think she'd ask you to come back if she didn't believe in you, no matter what you told her."

Both were silent for a while, watching the boys enjoy life without a care in the world except which one could swing the highest.

After a long moment, he asked the question that pressed hard on his mind. "What do you think Brooke will think of me when she learns the truth. Frankly, I wish she didn't have to know. And yet, I want her to know. What do I do?"

Usually, Ginger would advise him on almost any subject. But this time was different. "I can't answer that, Jake. It's a decision only you can make."

He nodded. He knew that. To blurt out the truth about his past would imply to Brooke that he thought there was, or could be, something personal between them. Wouldn't that be the height of presumption on his part? Shouldn't he first try and discover if there could be a personal relationship?

Knowing Ginger couldn't begin to answer his question, he muttered, "When is the right time to tell another person about your past? How much do you tell? When does withholding information become lying?"

thirteen

When Jake came to start on the agreed-upon repairs for the cottage, he brought Ginger's boys. Earlier on the phone, Brooke had told Ginger that would be fine, even helpful. Brooke and Ben went out to greet them. The boys immediately ran around back with Ben to play with Taz.

"Thought you might want this," Jake said, lifting a wire cage out of the truck bed. Brooke eyed the cage skeptically.

"It's a crate for Taz," he explained, realizing she wasn't pleased.

"You mean. . .lock him up?"

"A dog doesn't look at it that way," Jake explained. "It's a home, a safe haven for a dog. A place where it can feel protected. You just need to teach him to go home. Get some puppy food, and I'll show you."

Brooke went through the house to get the puppy food and took a handful out to Jake. He had placed the crate on the ground and began to demonstrate how to teach the puppy.

"Go home," he said and tossed a piece of dog food into the crate. Taz ran in, chomped on the piece of food while looking at them with big, soulful, black eyes in that werewolf face, then ran out. Jake repeated the exercise a couple more times, then addressed Ben. "Do that a few times during the day and at night when it's bedtime. He'll soon learn to go home whenever you say the words."

Brook tried to ignore the thought that came into her mind. How many times Bruce had said, "Don't run, don't yell so loud, don't track dirt in the house, no, you can't play in the rain, no, I can't play with you right now."

How different. This man was taking time to teach a little boy how to train a dog. How gratifying for a man to interact with a child instead of make demands.

But she shouldn't be comparing. That had been an entirely different lifestyle where appearances had to be a primary consideration. Bruce hadn't been abusive, just preoccupied with being an important politician. But was it any less important being a carpenter?

Her next thought startled her. Jesus had been a carpenter! Had He done work for people without pay to show His generosity? Had He been helpful like Jake? Had He stopped to speak to little children before tackling His work?

She felt He had.

An overwhelming urge to be kind to Jake swept over her. She could think of no reason whatsoever not to accept him as a friend, or at least as a friend of her son.

"Jake," she said and saw the light of surprise in his eyes before it quickly disappeared. An incredible look of pleasure settled on his face. Was that because she had called him by his first name? Perhaps. He obviously made an effort to have people like him and accept him as a Christian witness. *Do I not want the same? Didn't I spend many years feeling that I was not completely accepted by Bruce or his family, and didn't I wonder about his friends?*

She smiled. "Thanks for the crate and for teaching Taz to sit and lie down," she said. "He's really doing that for me and Ben. Watch!" Brooke reached into the bag for a few pieces of dog food. "Taz! Sit!" she commanded, holding the piece of food at his nose and moving it slightly over the puppy's head so he'd sit back.

Suddenly they all burst out laughing. Taz sat all right— right into his water bowl! And he stayed there.

Brooke gave him the dog food, patted him on the head, said, "Good boy," then turned an impish glance at Jake. She shrugged a shoulder. "Well, so now he has his own private bathtub."

❧

The ice was broken. Or at least it had begun to thaw from around Brooke's heart. The cottage was becoming transformed from a broken-down, neglected honeymoon cottage to a renovated, restored home for her and Ben.

On weekday evenings after work, Jake came and finished nailing down the roof shingles, cleaned out the gutters, tightened them against the house, and applied a coat of primer to the repaired corner.

On Saturday, he arrived early to scrape, patch, and fill any holes on the outside of the house, getting it and the porches ready for a fresh coat of paint.

Ginger came by to help Brooke put up the wallpaper border in Ben's room. They stood back to survey the effect of the dogs of all types running around the center of the walls. The walls themselves had not needed to be repainted. Brooke had simply given a basic washing to the cream-colored walls.

"Neat!" Ben exclaimed, excited about the dogs. "Taz loves it, Mom. Look!"

Taz really was loving the newspapers spotted with paint, and he began trying to chew them up.

After Ben obeyed her order to get the dog out of the room, Brooke turned to Ginger, saying proudly, "It's beginning to look like a boy's room."

Ginger shook her head, her brows making a furrow above her nose. "Not yet," she said. "You need to toss a shoe under the bed to join the dust-bunnies, make sure the bed's not made, open the bureau drawers, scatter toys all over the floor, sprinkle dirt—preferably wet—in several places, scribble a little crayon on the wall, and then you'll have yourself the ideal boy's room."

By the time Ginger finished, Brooke was laughing. What a joy this woman was! She mentally thanked God for Ginger's friendship. How rejuvenating to be reminded that she and her little boy didn't have to be perfect and that she didn't have to expect such behavior from her Ben. A house to live in was much more important than a house to look at.

Ginger took Ben and Taz home with her and the boys. Brooke finished up Ben's room. She hung the blue valances, put the matching spread on the bed, topped it with two red and white pillow cushions, dragged the box of toys out of the closet, neatly stacked some toys along with books on the bookshelf, and then mopped the hardwood floor. As soon as the floor dried, she dragged in his freshly vacuumed throw rug. Perfect! A wonderful room for a little boy to live in.

Around five o'clock, when Jake had just finished replacing broken rails in the banister, Ginger returned, bearing pizza.

At Brooke's insistence, they all came in to look at Ben's room and to exclaim over the new look before going out back to eat pizza. Brooke spread a blanket on the ground for the boys to sit on while they ate, trying to keep their pizza out of the range of Taz's mouth. Finally, Ben got puppy food and ordered Taz to "go home," which he did.

Brooke, Ginger, and Jake sat in kitchen chairs on the back porch. When Jake left to clean up from his repairs and put his tools in his truck, Ginger left with her boys, saying they all had to have baths and get to bed early since tomorrow was Sunday.

When Jake was about ready to leave, Brooke went out to say good-bye.

Ben stood looking up at Jake. "You wanna teach Taz some more tricks?" he asked.

Taz was tugging on the bottom of Jake's jeans, as if he, too, didn't want Jake to leave. Brooke realized she felt a little lonely each evening when he left.

"He's been here all day, Ben," Brooke said.

"I don't mind, if you don't," Jake said.

She shook her head. "I don't."

Jake smiled broadly, as if he were in no hurry to go. He commanded Taz to sit, which he did, while looking up soulfully, waiting for his food. Jake simply patted him on the head and said, "Good boy."

Taz continued to sit, giving the impression he preferred food to a pat.

"If you have a leash, we can take him for a walk and teach him to heel," Jake told Ben, which sent the boy off like a flash.

"It might seem cruel to keep Taz on a leash," Jake said. "But it's best for him when you first begin to teach him. This is a smart dog. And he's strong-willed. Before long, he'll try to take over as the leader of the pack. If you tell him to sit and he wanders off, you've lost it. Keep him on a leash when training. He'll learn the commands and obey them after he's off the leash. Also, when you take him for a walk, keep him on the leash.

Brooke soon learned what he meant by a strong-willed puppy.

They took Taz for a walk along a nearby bicycle path that ran along through the trees. Jake was teaching her how to make him heel when they walked the dog. It wasn't too hard for Ben, since he was closer to the ground than Brooke, which meant he was closer to the dog's mouth with the food.

Jake even did all right at keeping Taz at his left heel while reaching over, behind his left leg, with an occasional piece of dog food.

When Brooke tried it, she felt awkward holding the leash with her left hand while stooping down and reaching across herself with a bite of rewarding food.

More awkward than that were Ben's words when he blurted out enthusiastically, "We look just like a family, don't we, Mom?"

Flustered, she looked away from Jake. When she did, she straightened from her cramped, sideways, leaning-over position. Her hand moved around in front of her, and Taz followed it, coming after the food. He came across the front of her legs, then ran around to the other side, wrapping the leash around her legs. Then he began to pull on the leash, tightening its hold on her.

"Oh, yes, we're like a family," Brooke spouted, trying to keep her balance. "The man and boy laugh at the woman who gets tied up by a dog! Just like a couple of men!" She struggled to get a piece of dog food in Taz's mouth so that he would stay still, hoping she could keep her balance. "Help me!" she demanded.

Jake and Ben grinned at each other, but Jake came over, stood for an instant very close, his warm twinkling eyes looking into her irate ones for a long moment. He took the leash from her hand, then unwrapped her and gave the leash to Ben.

"Food," he said, and Brooke gladly slapped her handful of food into his outstretched hand.

"I can do it," Ben said confidently.

Jake still grinned, giving her a sly glance. "Got all tied up in knots, huh?"

She gave him a warning look, then watched as Ben executed the command and reward quite well.

She was thinking, *Yes, tied in knots in more ways than one and for many reasons.* Ben said they looked like a family. Maybe someday she could put the past behind her and get her life straightened out enough to consider something like that. She wanted it to be right this time. When she thought about it or when it entered her mind unbidden, the ideal man began to look suspiciously like Jake Randolph.

৯

Each evening during the following week, Jake painted the front porch and the shutters a deep gray. On Saturday he brought two crew members and a retired house painter from church who volunteered to help singles. By Saturday evening the cottage looked like a new house.

After all the men except Jake left, Brooke and Ben stood with him, surveying his handiwork.

"Cool!" Ben exclaimed.

"Oh, Jake, it is beautiful," Brooke said, looking at the soft, dove gray cottage with its darker trim and gleaming white banister. It didn't look like a broken-down honeymoon cottage anymore. It was a rejuvenated home for a mother and her son.

"I'll have to get shrubs and plant flowers below the banister," Brooke said and asked Jake if he had any suggestions.

"We're clearing land around the church where a new conference center and housing is being built. There are some azaleas that we have to take out and have permission to give away. I can bring several of those," he offered.

"That would be perfect," she said. "And I'll get some

pansies. We'll just have a riot of color." She could almost see the finished product. A background of blooming azaleas, or just the green leaves, bordered by splashes of yellow, maroon, purple, blue, and white. Yes, it was beginning to shape up.

She was beginning to enjoy the present and look ahead with anticipation, instead of dwelling on the past.

Sunday at church proved that to her more strongly.

Since that first Sunday, Ginger and her boys always saved room in their pew for Brooke and Ben. Jake usually sat at the end of the pew, next to Mike. This Sunday, at the end of the worship service, the congregation took communion. The pastor related briefly the meaning of the Lord's Supper and reminded the listeners that Jesus died to take away the sins of the world.

Brooke felt that she was rededicating herself, making a new commitment to live closer to the Lord as she partook, but she had to tell Ben he couldn't participate. Her son was close to six years old. She must make as her first priority Ben's religious training. If she succeeded in every area but failed to clearly teach God's love for him and the salvation that was offered through Jesus, then she would fail totally as a parent.

With determination and a feeling of well-being, Brooke joined in with the voices and was able to hear Jake's baritone as they sang the closing song, "Blest be the tie that binds our hearts in Christian love."

She was humming the song as she leaned over to pick up her Bible and purse from underneath the pew in front of her. She straightened up and turned toward Ben, but her glance met Jake's gaze. Their eyes held for a moment. He smiled in a way that had begun to affect her heart in unexpected ways.

How could anyone not respect him? Admire him? But. . . love?

But. . .the song is referring to Christian love. That's entirely different from the physical love between a man and woman, isn't it? she asked herself, ignoring her rapid heartbeat. She brushed at her cheek as if to erase the warmth she felt rising to her face.

She quickly lowered her gaze to Ben. "You have all your papers?" she asked, reminding herself that other "ties that bind" had for a long time held a negative connotation in her life.

In spite of her fears, however, was her heart binding with Jake's? And much as she might try to dismiss her feelings as Christian love, if she were honest, didn't they hold something else as well?

fourteen

Jake had heard Ginger complain that during her last months of pregnancy, time had dragged interminably, almost stopped. That's what time seemed to be doing for him. He kept busy and looked forward to the evenings and Saturdays he could spend at Brooke's, and ever-present on his mind was that he had four months, three weeks to go until his probation was over. Then it was four months, two weeks. Four months, one week. Four months.

But the time dragged. Could he keep letting his feelings grow for Brooke without telling her the truth of his past? Shouldn't he find out if she thought there was a chance for them together? Suppose she said there was a chance and asked him to meet her parents in Indiana?

He'd have to say, "Sorry. I wouldn't be allowed to go out of state just to meet someone's parents." Now what kind of relationship could be built on that kind of information?

❧

There was no denying to Brooke's mind that Jake had become, to say the least, a friend. She was not indifferent to him and could not pretend so. But a man like him deserved a woman who was as openly committed to the Lord as he. She determined to follow through with her renewed dedication to the Lord.

She decided that Ben should memorize some basic verses from the Bible. The first and most important to her was John 3:16. She had him repeat each phrase every morning, and by

105

the end of the week, she figured it should be a part of him. To her delight, he could say it verbatim by Wednesday morning.

That's the morning she decided it was time to get her body in shape. She wasn't overweight, but she knew her body wasn't toned the way it should be. She would give water aerobics a try. She, Ben, and Taz showed up at Ginger's before 10:00 A.M.

Ginger and the boys were delighted to see them. As soon as the children gathered at the side of the pool, Ben asked, "Hey, you guys want to hear me say John 3:16?"

"I do!" Danny said, and they all stood quietly while Ben recited it.

"For God so loved the world, that he gave his only begotten son, that whosoever believeth in him, should not perish, but have everlasting life."

Mike tousled Ben's hair like Brooke had seen Jake do. "That's really good, Ben," he said. He looked over and grinned at his mother, who nodded her approval of him. It was beautiful how those two communicated with just a glance.

Other women began to arrive. She met a middle-aged neighbor of Ginger's and her friend; a fourth-grade school teacher; two overweight women trying to get fit; a trim writer who said she needed the exercise since she sat at her computer from 6:00 A.M. until time for aerobics, pausing only for a quick breakfast; an older woman; and two single parents who shared an apartment. One worked the second shift as a nurse and the other worked as a waitress. The nurse brought her two daughters, ages six and four, and the other woman brought her daughter, age eight.

Mike drew a hopscotch outline on the concrete with sidewalk chalk, and the children began to play, except for the four-year-old girl who wanted to swing. Her six-year-old sister had to keep running over to push her little sister. The children had to be careful not to stumble over Taz, who was right on the heels of whomever's turn it was to jump. He liked to pick up the pebble and take it away, too. The children enjoyed the puppy's antics.

All the women were ready to get into the pool by 10:00. Brooke was not surprised at Ginger's expertise. She called, "Straight-leg kick while moving the opposite arm toward the opposite leg."

The worst thing about it was watching that the children, mimicking their mothers, did the exercises with such ease. To Brooke's relief, they soon became bored with that and returned to their own games.

While exercising, the women talked about themselves between listening to Ginger give commands. The singles talked about their difficulties, the older woman about her age, and the heavy ones about their weight.

"Fanny kick while pushing the water toward yourself. Heel kick behind and touch the heel with the opposite hand, then heel kick in front," Ginger commanded. "Leap frog" was next, and Brooke could feel her body moving in ways she hadn't imagined. But, she could tell, wet exercise was much more pleasant than dry exercise.

They ran in the water, then checked their pulses. Her heartbeat had definitely accelerated by the third round. The toning part was what she liked best, wrapping her arms around a noodle to keep herself afloat and working the leg and tummy muscles. After a cool-down of stretching and finally hugging themselves while taking deep breaths and exhaling, Brooke felt like every muscle in her body had been massaged—and it felt very good!

After an hour, the women dried off. Some slipped on T-shirts over their suits, and some left in their suits with a towel slung around their shoulders.

"Stay a while," Ginger said to Brooke as she was drying off.

After the others left, Ginger invited Brooke and Ben to lunch, which turned out to be peanut butter and banana sandwiches. Carrot sticks again. Juice for the children. Brooke and Ginger had lemonade, then went out onto the porch with coffee.

"This is really a nice place, Ginger," Brooke complimented. She laughed. "For adults, too."

Ginger nodded. "Thanks to my parents, I have it. Jake and I were raised here. My parents bought it years ago before the island was built up, so they got it for a real bargain. Then they built a new house in Bluffton and rented this out to me and Leo." She lifted her eyes and brows toward heaven. "That's my ex-husband. You wanna hear about a real skunk?"

Brooke grinned and nodded. She really did. She wanted to know how Ginger could be so warm, friendly, and well-adjusted with all her responsibilities.

"Well, it's like this," Ginger began her story. Leo Harris was raised on the golf course. In his younger days, he was a caddy to a famous golfer. He was away on the golf circuit almost all the time. He said he wanted a big family, but he must have meant he wanted her to have a big family while he traveled everywhere. Ginger had tried to understand. After all, he was their meal ticket. But it began to seem that he was away when he should have been home.

Finally, Leo claimed it wasn't fair to her and the boys for them to wait for him to come home, and the boys didn't seem to know him. Baby Danny cried when Leo came near because he didn't know his dad. Leo was a golf instructor for a while and could have stayed with it if he'd wanted to make a living and take care of a family. But he enjoyed hobnobbing with the pros and then decided he wanted to be one of them.

"He's now on the golf circuit and making good money," Ginger said. "He pays alimony and child support. That eases his conscience, and the children think it's great that he's a golf pro and sends them presents." She threw up her hands. "That's his way. Make a big splash. Be noticed. But everyday living with and caring for a family is not part of the picture."

Brooke could understand. "Bruce didn't want to be tied down either," she said. "We were very happy for three months." She felt she could confide in Ginger, and the prospect of doing so suddenly seemed freeing. She'd held back so long and hadn't even told her parents everything.

"Ours was a whirlwind romance," Brooke said. "I was in my second year of nurse's training when he returned from law school, ready to become part of a big law firm."

Brooke told about working at Haddon's Department Store and doing some modeling for them. Bruce had seen her model before, but he said she'd grown up in the past couple of years. He called her a real beauty and swept her off her feet by taking her out of her ordinary life and involving her in his dreams of grandeur.

"To the public," she said, "I lived a charmed life as the wife of Bruce Haddon, handsome young state senator." They were occasional visitors at the governor's mansion and attended political fund-raising dinners at the Haddons's. Photographs were taken and used to publicize Bruce with his model-wife impeccably dressed and made-up and his adorable young son.

"But our private life was entirely different," Brooke revealed. "He didn't want a child so soon in his career. Nor did he want a wife who refused to leave her son with a nanny and go on the campaign trail with him. When things got worse, I wanted to return to nurses' training, but he forbade it."

Tears came to Brooke's eyes as she revealed those painful years. The more public acceptance Bruce received, the worse he became in his private life. He became verbally abusive, unfaithful, controlling, and destroyed her self-esteem and ignored his son every day.

"Our marriage was over a long time ago," Brooke said. "But a little over a year ago when I walked away from Bruce's funeral, I knew his lover was being buried on the other side of town. They ran into a concrete median strip. The car flipped over, and the gasoline tank exploded. Tests proved their blood-alcohol content was above the legal limit."

She looked beyond, distantly. "I cried; I grieved for six years of a failing marriage, for a son without a father, for truth that will have to be told someday, for all I had lost—my livelihood and my self-esteem."

Ginger spoke distantly. "Jake has helped me regain some of my self-esteem," she admitted. "But I don't know if I will ever shake the feeling of failure and guilt. God is healing me, but it's not easy losing a husband and knowing your children have lost a father." She raised her voice on the next words. "Even if he was a skunk!"

"At least I have a roof over my head," Brooke said, realizing she was more blessed than many. "And Bruce's parents said to let them know if we need anything, but they seemed to blame me for the failed marriage. Somehow, I hadn't been the kind of wife I should have been. I think they expected me to live up to the image I portrayed on the runway as a model. But Ginger, that was a youthful body, professional hair stylist, gorgeous clothes, and enough makeup to cover any blemish. That's not me at all. I'm a small-town girl with basic values."

She sighed. "At least, I used to be. The more I needed God in my life, the more I pulled away from Him."

"I know exactly what you mean, Brooke. Not that the Lord causes it, but He sure can use our failures to get our attention. When you take a good long look at what's important in life, you discover it's not all those things the world can provide. Basically, the things God provides, like purpose and meaning and love, are the things that last."

Brooke nodded. "I was raised to know those things. But it was head knowledge only. I'm realizing how important family life is, and friends. You have helped me so much, Ginger, by being a friend. And Jake's attitude about serving others is admirable. I'd like to volunteer to do what I can to help some way. I know I haven't been to their nightly meetings yet, but maybe I could help with the single moms some way." She shrugged. "I can identify with them."

"Ah, perfect!" Ginger exclaimed. "We can always use help there. As a matter of fact, Evelyn just moved into her own place."

"Ben's teacher?"

"That's the one."

"Oh, she's nice," Brooke said. "I'd love to do what I can to help."

"Great. Hers is one of the older homes on the island and is in much worse shape than yours ever thought of being. Let's go tomorrow and help her clean."

Brooke threw back her head and laughed.

"What's so funny, girl?" Ginger wanted to know.

"I was just thinking. In Indiana, I had my own housekeeper. Now, I get a kick out of thinking about going to Evelyn's and cleaning her house when mine is still under construction."

Ginger nodded. "If I waited until I had my own life

straightened out before I helped another person, I'd never get anything done."

Brooke studied her for a moment, then asked seriously. "Is that what makes you so happy, Ginger? Helping others?"

"That's part of it. But it started when I decided I couldn't handle my own life and gave it to the Lord. I began to use His Word as my road map instead of making up my own. It works. And the more I try to give of myself without expecting anything in return, the blessings just come. Like with you, Brooke. I was just trying to be friendly and let you know that Jake wasn't some kind of ogre, and I'm ending up with a strong friendship between us." She looked over at Brooke and asked tentatively, "You don't still think Jake's an ogre, do you?"

"Of course not," she said. "He's a good worker and a fine Christian." She stood quickly, lest her face reveal what she felt in her heart. "Now, I'd better go and buy some sandwich makings if we're going 'foot washing' tomorrow."

୬

When they arrived at Evelyn's the next day, Brooke reprimanded herself a dozen times. All went well at first, and Evelyn was so grateful for the visit, the lunch, and the offers to help. Then she began telling Ginger how great Jake was.

"Jake brought me those azaleas," she said, taking them out front to show them. "And he planted them."

Jake had told Brooke he was helping clear land at the church for a new center to be built and he'd offered to bring her some azaleas that the church didn't want.

He hasn't brought mine yet came Brooke's immediate thought, and she was shocked by what felt like a strong case of jealousy. But how could she possibly be jealous when she didn't even want a man in her life? Did she?

Maybe it was just that Evelyn seemed to be harping on the

same subject. Jake had come by her place several evenings after work, and she showed them where he had torn out the bottom of the cabinet beneath the sink where pipes had leaked and rotted out the wood. He was going to replace it. And he was going to do it free of charge.

With her adrenaline flowing and trying to control her attitude, Brooke scrubbed the inside and outside of the kitchen cabinets that were in reasonable shape and would be fine for use if the shelves were covered with shelf paper. With Ginger being as much a workaholic as Jake, the kitchen took shape within a few hours while the boys and Evelyn's seven-year-old daughter played out back. The windows sparkled, the walls were stripped of old, peeling paper, and the ceiling was cleaned. Ginger talked about patching the holes in the wall so someone could either paint or paper later on.

"Jake does that kind of thing, doesn't he?" Evelyn asked.

"Yep," Ginger said. "But so do I."

Brooke got the strong impression that Evelyn would prefer Jake to do the job.

Well, what did I expect? Brooke asked herself. *Did I think I was the only recipient of Jake's water-basin principle? What's wrong with me? Where's my Christian spirit?*

fifteen

"Does she ever mention me?" Jake asked in what he hoped sounded like a casual question while he sat at Ginger's kitchen table and ate his late supper. "I mean my work or anything?"

"Who?" Ginger asked, feigning innocence.

Jake gave her a hard look. "Who were we talking about?"

Ginger wrinkled her brow, as if trying to think. "Brooke and Evelyn?"

"Exactly," he said, knowing his sister was playing games with him. "You were telling me about your and Brooke's visit to Evelyn's."

"Oh, yes," she said. "She talked about you almost the whole time."

Jake kept chewing and staring at Ginger. This wasn't funny. But that silly little grin on her face indicated that she thought it was.

"Okay," she said. "Evelyn did. She praised you for bringing the azaleas, planting them, repairing the cabinets—free of charge!" Ginger lifted her eyebrows. "Brooke didn't say a word."

Jake pushed his plate away and sighed. Now, how was he supposed to handle this? How could he keep Brooke from thinking he was interested in another woman, without letting her know he was interested in her? Could he act uninterested for three more months, then tell her it was all some kind of waiting game?

"I've sure got myself in some kind of pickle," he ground out.

Ginger gently rested her hand on his arm. "Just tell her how you feel, Jake," she said softly.

He didn't have to ask if she meant Evelyn or Brooke.

❧

Jake knew he couldn't "just tell her how he felt." He'd have to reveal his past first. But before doing that, he had to have some indication she could care about him in a personal way. One couldn't just blurt out, "Hey, look, I've sinned, and you need to know it. I spent time in prison where I got my life on track with God. Now I'm a practicing Christian, so accept me."

No, he knew it wasn't that easy. It hadn't been easy to admit to himself he'd been a deliberate sinner. It was much harder admitting it to a woman he cared about. But it had to be done if he expected to have any kind of close relationship with Brooke.

First, however, he'd have to have some indication she was ready for a relationship. And if so, with him!

And too, how could he expect a classy, beautiful woman like her to give him the time of day? She'd been real nice to him lately, but was it because of himself, or because he was her repairman? Or because he was the brother of Ginger? She didn't have anything against him, but did that mean she had anything for him?

Didn't he have to make sure she knew him and trusted him? After all, they hadn't known each other very long. She was trying to get a handle on her life. It took Ginger a couple of years after Leo left before she could shake her bitterness and turn it over to the Lord. Even then, she had to take baby steps before she learned to walk through life with joy and confidence.

He smiled to himself. Now, Ginger was running with the kind of endurance the Good Book spoke about.

The best he could do at the time was simply let Brooke get to know him better. He took her azaleas on Saturday—and planted them. He'd like to tell her that the reason he went to Evelyn's on weekdays and Brooke's on Saturdays was because he had more hours to spend with Brooke if he went on Saturday, but he couldn't blurt that out. So he got on his hands and knees beside her in the flower beds.

He loved the way she dug her hands into the rich soil, not even mentioning the fact that the dirt got under her finger-nails. She just laughed happily and said, "My in-laws' gardener did all the planting and landscaping at out house in Indiana. But I love doing this. Getting my hands in the dirt. Getting down to earth, I guess you'd call it."

Jake's heart beat fast against his chest as he looked over at her happy face so close to his. She had a little smudge of dirt on her cheek, strangely making her even more appealing. He warned himself that it was the dirt that put the joyful look on her face—not him!

So he discussed the plants. "The pansies like acid soil," he said, pushing the dirt around them. "So do azaleas. The two will thrive well together." *As we could*, he added in his mind and hoped he wouldn't blurt that out.

He liked the way she looked at him with appreciation when the beds turned out beautifully, then when he pruned off the dead and damaged leaf stalks from the trunks of the palms, giving them a tidy, healthy look.

He could easily have told her how much he enjoyed work-ing on her household projects, asking her opinion, talking to Ben, training Taz. All that had begun to mean more to him than he could have imagined.

She was even receptive to his suggestion when he said, "You might want to consider putting a fence out back. Taz is getting mighty big, and he'll be shedding a lot of that long hair before long."

She gave him a wry glance. "He's already passed the twenty-pound mark—by six pounds." Shaking her head, she added, "That was supposed to be our little miniature puppy."

Brooke had already been finding a lot of black hair floating around. She definitely would consider a fence. Especially now that the inside of the house was getting fixed up.

It took another week and all day Saturday for him to take care of the living-room floor. When he'd looked under the moldy corner of the carpet, he not only discovered some ruined boards but that the rest of the floor was a beautiful hardwood. He suggested getting rid of the carpet and refinishing the floor. Brooke agreed.

"I'm not the greatest cook in the world," Brooke said when he began work on the floor, "but I fixed enough supper for all of us if you'd like to join us."

He sat down and ate with them beneath that dark-spotted kitchen ceiling. The conversation centered around the repairs, Ben, and Taz. Jake couldn't imagine that anyone would not love that little boy, with such winning ways, and even the werewolf-looking puppy who sat with big black eyes looking soulfully from one to the other, hoping for people-food which Ben couldn't resist sneaking to him.

Yes, Jake decided definitely. The time had come to find some answers for himself.

⤞

It was Ginger who presented the opportunity when she suggested they all go to Harbour Town on Saturday, instead of working. Telling himself not to be apprehensive about it, Jake broached the subject after he finished working on Brooke's floor Friday night.

He spoke as casually as he could. "We're all going to Harbour Town on Saturday. Ginger wanted to do some shopping, and I plan to take the boys on a boat ride to watch the dolphins. Would you and Ben like to go along?"

Brooke was glad Jake chose a time to mention it when Ben wasn't close. Otherwise, it would be hard to say no. It sounded like a wonderful outing. "We wouldn't want to impose," she said.

He smiled. "I asked you," he said. "And Ginger is going to call you. So if you want, just save your answer until Ginger calls. Good night, Brooke. I'll run around and say good-bye to Ben before I go."

"Thanks for the invitation," she said as he hastened around the corner of the house.

By the time Ginger called, Brooke had decided it would be a lovely outing for the two of them. She'd love to go shopping with Ginger. Ben would love to go out on a boat and watch the dolphins.

Early Saturday morning, Ginger picked Brooke and Ben up in her van. Jake had driven, alone, in his truck. The boys were greatly excited about the excursion. All three of Ginger's boys were filling Ben in on all they would see and that the dolphins would jump sky-high, maybe jump right into the boat. Ben was fascinated just looking at all the yachts, sailboats, and fishing charters in the harbor.

Brooke was most fascinated by the brilliant red geraniums covering the entire length of a long row of shops. People sat in rocking chairs, looking out across a sea of red geraniums, while other people walked a couple of feet below, along the walkway between the shops and harbor. Amid the geraniums stood live oaks. Hanging from the awnings were baskets laden with brilliant red geraniums.

One could move the chairs back under the shade of the awning or pull them beyond the awning into the warmth of the sunshine and look out over the red geraniums, the walkway below, out to the ships in the harbor, and the sparkling blue water beyond.

"The most famous attraction here," Ginger said, after Jake and the boys had left on the boat, "is the candy-striped lighthouse. There's a great gift shop at the top. But let's start here and work our way around, okay?"

"Okay," Brooke said, looking around at the quaint area, patterned after a Mediterranean fishing village. The two women walked along the boards beneath a yellow awning. Brooke bought a T-shirt with leaping dolphins printed on it for Ben. In one of the shops she bought him swimming trunks.

After a couple hours of shopping and sightseeing, Ginger pointed out some of the quaint restaurants, but they all planned to eat lunch together after the guys returned. They sat in the rockers along the edge of the boards, in front of the long row of shops, where they could look out at the harbor, looking at the sailboats, yachts, pelicans, and sunshine.

"Over there's the famous Liberty Oak tree," Ginger said. "Sometimes there is live entertainment beneath it. Also there are spectacular sunsets here."

"This is so peaceful," Brooke said. "I could sit here and rock forever. Oh," she said, looking to her right, "he has the right idea."

Ginger laughed, looking over at the sculpture of a man sitting on a timber, resting his feet on another timber. His elbows were propped on his thighs. He had a sandwich in one hand and a book in another. "The sculpture is called 'Out-to-Lunch,'" she said.

Brooke rocked gently with her arms on the rocker arms, basking in the warmth and beauty of this spectacular setting. "I don't think I've relaxed since I've been here," she said. "I need this."

"Yep," Ginger agreed. "We should always take time to smell the roses." She looked over at Brooke and grinned. "Or the geraniums." Her smile faded and she grew serious. "You know, Brooke, I really value your friendship. A lot of the single moms think they can't relate to me because I'm not strapped for money. I do have a lot," she admitted. "But we live on alimony and child support and rely on my brother for repairs and plumbing and roofing. I do the water aerobics to make a little money of my own and give myself a feeling of independence and contributing."

"It looks to me like you're contributing double as a parent. Remember, I'm without a husband too."

"Right, but the world doesn't always see it our way. Anyhow, I'm planning to take computer and accounting courses after Danny starts school. When Jake moves out and all the boys are in school, the way Jake's business is booming, I can keep books for Jake and take his calls. He has an answering service now. I can do all that at home."

"Jake is moving out?" Brooke asked.

"I expect him to one of these days. He could have moved in with Mom and Dad, um, but, I. . .uh, he moved in with me to help with the kids. Anyway, I mean he will want a place of his own one of these days. You know, marriage and children and all those good things?"

Brook wondered why that so startled her heart. It suddenly dawned on her how much and how quickly Jake Randolph had invaded her and Ben's lives. And his presence was no longer unwelcome. Were he and Evelyn serious about each other? "He's. . .getting married?" she asked.

"Oh, no," Ginger said. "He doesn't have any definite plans."

"But he's going with someone?"

"Not at the moment."

"I would think a fine man like Jake would have married long ago."

Ginger shook her head. "Nope. He's never been married." She stood and gazed out over the water. "About time they returned, I think."

"Oh, are they late?" Brooke said, feeling an instant of concern.

Ginger looked at her watch. "No. It'll be thirty more minutes or so. Let's go get something to drink."

Brooke knew that Ginger had deliberately changed the subject from talking about Jake. As they walked past the shops, Ginger kept pointing out items of interest, but Brooke's mind was on Jake. Why had Ginger said he had a choice of moving in with his parents or her? Where had he lived before that? Had he lived with. . .someone? Had he lost someone? Her curiosity was piqued. Why was Ginger so open and aboveboard about everything—except Jake?

❧

The boat trip turned out to be a major success. Especially for Ben. He'd seen dolphins jump sky-high and thought they might even jump into the boat, but they didn't, and he loved his T-shirt and insisted upon putting it on right then, tag and all. He intended to sleep in it that night.

"Jake knows all about alligators," Ben reported. "He said, sometime, if you let me, we can go see some."

"We'll see," Brooke answered, and Jake, taking the hint,

said they needed to find some lunch for those boys.

"I have an idea," Ginger said. "Why don't we buy some sandwiches and go out for a picnic on the property?"

Brooke had no idea what the property was, but there seemed to be a challenge in Ginger's eyes as she and her brother gave each other a long look before he grinned and said, "Great idea."

As it turned out, the picnic spot was a couple of acres of oceanfront property in a section of fine homes in Sea Pines. Beneath a couple of live oaks, dripping with Spanish moss, sat a picnic table like the one in Ginger's back yard. The beautifully landscaped land, with its spectacular view of the ocean, boasted its own private walkway leading to the beach.

Brooke knew a bunch of people with four rowdy boys didn't come to places like this for an outing unless they had a friend who owned it or owned it themselves. "Whose is this?" she asked curiously, looking from Ginger to Jake, while the boys frolicked around the trees, searching for alligators.

Jake's grin said it all, while Ginger spread out the quilt she'd taken from his truck. "I've been buying it for several years," he said. "And as soon as we finish the house we're working on, I'll be close to having it paid off."

Well, she guessed Jake's business was doing all right. "It's wonderful," Brooke said, impressed.

"Thanks," he answered. "And being a builder, I think I could manage to put up a pretty good house." He added, with a grin, "At cost."

"I'll just bet you could," Brooke said, nodding and smiling. Now she could see why Ginger mentioned his moving out of her house. After it was paid for, he'd probably build. But no matter how beautiful, wouldn't he be lonely. . .alone?

sixteen

The following Friday evening Jake announced that he was going to take Ginger's boys out to the lagoon on Saturday to see alligators. Now that warmer weather had come, the gators would be lying in the sun.

"Could Ben come along?" he asked.

"He's wanted to do that since before we came here when an alligator was mentioned, but frankly, that frightens me. You see how active he is. And with four boys for you to watch. . ."

Brooke heard the edge in his voice when he asked, "Don't you know I wouldn't put that boy in danger?"

She looked at him. For a long instant their gazes held. "I know," she said. "I'm just overly protective, I guess."

"That's not so bad," he said softly. "But you can trust me."

She caught her breath for a moment. She had the feeling he was not just talking about trusting him with Ben.

She nodded. "I do trust you, Jake."

His smile was warm. "Good. Then if the gators don't eat us, how about my taking you out to dinner tomorrow evening?"

Strangely, his quip about the gators eating them didn't disturb her nearly as much as his asking her out to dinner.

"Well, I guess you do deserve a good dinner after eating my cooking all week."

"The food was fine," he said. "The company exceptional."

"Well, yeah," she said, trying to hide her unexpected elation, "Ben's a great dinner companion. I assume you're inviting him too?"

"Not this time," he said. "I've already talked to Ginger. He can stay over there. After all, the boys will need to do a lot of gator talk."

Of course Brooke knew his reason for asking her out, without Ben, could be to discuss church trips or activities. There were many for children, and she'd already learned that Jake never asked about an outing in front of Ben, instead asking her discreetly when the boy wasn't right there. And too, Ginger could have mentioned to her brother Brooke's intention of getting more involved with singles. Jake could have some possible ways for her to get involved that he wanted to discuss, since he was actively involved with singles—like repairing her house. . .and Evelyn's house.

So this wasn't necessarily personal. "Should I dress up or go casual?" she asked, hoping her voice sounded the latter.

"What about Fitzgerald's? Anything goes there. From dressy to casual."

Fitzgerald's. She and Bruce had gone there on their honeymoon. They had dressed up.

"I'd like to go casual," she said, and Jake nodded.

ℯℯ

This is casual? Jake asked himself when he came to pick Brooke up. He'd brought Ben and the boys by so Brooke could see that the gators hadn't eaten her son, hadn't even bitten him, in fact. Then he'd taken them all, and Taz, to Ginger's. After he'd showered, shampooed, and dressed in slacks and knit shirt, he'd driven the SUV to Brooke's.

He knocked on the front screen, and she was there immediately. As soon as she stepped out on the porch, he felt anything but casual. She looked anything but casual, although she wore white slacks and a sea-green silk blouse that turned her eyes the color of warm summertime, a place where one might wish to bask forever. Her eyes were fringed with long brown lashes, and her soft lips were tinted coral. Tiny gold earrings gleamed at her ears. He'd seen her dressed stylishly with her hair down to her shoulders at church, but the rest of the week she'd worn jeans or shorts and had pulled her hair back into a ponytail.

This evening, it was different. She'd dressed for him. She'd let her hair down for him. She was having dinner with him.

There was nothing casual about the two of them going out for dinner together. This was his first date in three years. For her, it was probably the first since before she married, more than seven years ago. Casual? Tonight, that word had nothing at all to do with how one dressed.

Was tonight the time for him to reveal his past? His silent prayer was for God's leadership on what to say, how to say it, and when to say it.

But for now, he wanted nothing to intrude upon this special time. Surely God wouldn't have brought this wonderful woman into his life without reason. Surely! No, God was not cruel.

They'd barely had time to begin discussing the alligator day before they arrived at Fitzgerald's, only a few minutes away.

Jake had been to the restaurant several times. He'd brought Ginger here for her birthday when his mom and dad had come up from Bluffton to stay with the boys. He'd come with a group of singles from church one time. He'd brought Meagan here when they first started going together. He knew, most likely, Brooke had been here.

"Have you been here before?" he asked.

She nodded. "Bruce and I came here on our honeymoon. I

think we sat in the main dining room over there."

"We'd like a table by the windows, if we could," Jake said when the maitre d' came to seat them.

The maitre d' led the way down the narrow carpeted section with long narrow windows on one side and seated them at one of the many tables-for-two. On the other side, divided by a low brick wall and brick columns, were long planters filled with green ferns and vines. Green shutters were pushed aside, revealing the main dining room. The walls, carpeting, and tablecloths were in a subdued maroon and green hue. Dim light glowed from the Tiffany chandeliers, and on each table a candle glowed in a silver goblet, surrounded by a frosted globe.

Jake gave the maitre d' a grateful glance when he seated them at a table where they could look out the window into the courtyard.

"Oh, this is nice," Brooke exclaimed, looking out.

In the courtyard, groupings of small cast-iron tables, some for four, some for two, sectioned off by flowering purple and white azalea hedges, sat on fine white gravel. A cocoa palm, with its spiked branches making it as wide as it was tall, was draped gracefully with small white lights. This was flanked by tall palmettos. Surrounding the courtyard were other palmettos and large wooden planters spilling over with ferns and vines.

"This really is lovely," Brooke said, and Jake smiled.

They ordered the same thing—combination seafood platter of scallops, shrimp, and flounder. "I'll have mine fried," Brooke said, thinking she'd have to make sure and do some extra walking besides her three mornings of water aerobics.

"Same here," Jake said.

Brooke ordered the raspberry vinaigrette dressing for her

green salad and Jake ordered blue cheese. They drank iced tea while Jake asked her how she liked living on the island.

Brooke looked down at her glass and ran a finger around the rim, a small reflective smile on her lips. Bruce had never asked her how she liked the island. He had been very romantic and sweet, but the focus of attention never left himself. She realized now that was because of the way he was raised—an only son with every opportunity, expected to achieve. He hadn't been bad or mean to her—just full of himself.

Now she looked across at Jake and thought how romantic it was to have a man ask about herself, rather than try and impress her with himself. She could hardly believe she was sitting here at a small table-for-two in the light of a candle, across from a handsome man, appealing to her in an even stronger way than when they worked together in the yard. This was like being on a date for the first time, and she had to remind herself that it wasn't necessarily a real date.

"I like it here very much," she said, "now that I'm beginning to understand the island. To use Ben's word, it's really 'neat' how the island is shaped like a shoe. So if someone tells me a store is located in the heel or the toes, I know what they mean."

Their laughter was soft and friendly as they propped their arms on the table, leaning toward each other as they talked. "And the sole of the shoe," Jake said, "is a twelve-mile beach."

The food came and was delicious. Brooke talked about her parents and Jake about his. When they finished eating, neither wanted dessert. Jake suggested they have coffee in the courtyard.

They sat at a small cast-iron table, surrounded by the array of azalea hedges. The hot coffee was the perfect balance to an evening with a slight chill in the air. A full silvery moon rose in the deep blue-gray sky, brushed gently by a whisk of cloud like a smudge of cotton candy.

The evening seemed so perfect. They got along so well, and she felt there wasn't a pretentious bone in his body, which appealed to her. She smiled at him. Maybe this was a real date after all. She liked the restaurant, the food, and their walking out into the courtyard. Brooke reached up to feel the texture of the moss hanging from the oaks.

"It's so graceful," she commented. "We don't have Spanish moss in Indiana. How do they get it to hang like that?"

"It isn't Spanish at all," Jake said. "And it has no roots. It's an air plant."

"Is it a parasite?"

"Nope," Jake said. "It just dangles freely, getting its nourishment from the rain and the sun. But the downside is, it attracts little red bugs called chiggers. Believe me, they itch."

Brooke jerked her hand down and grimaced.

Jake laughed, but could have kicked his backside for that remark. This was to be a romantic night where they could relate on a strictly personal level, and he had to bring up the subject of chiggers. Great going, Jake!

He exhaled after a deep breath and suggested they walk on the beach.

They walked up the timber steps, along the concrete and oyster shell walkway, and onto the timber boardwalk leading to the beach, passing sea oats, low growing cocoa palms, and tall palmettos.

Brooke took off her sandals and spoke of the warm, white sand feeling so good on her feet and between her toes. She looked up at the full moon and spoke of the beauty of its reflection casting a silver shadow on the blue water. The night was perfect. Just cool enough that she wondered if it might seem natural for him to put his arm around her shoulders or hold her hand.

❧

Jake wondered if he dared reach for her hand. Maybe he could tell her how he'd come to care for her in such a special way. Surely, this night meant more than friendship to her, as it did to him. Maybe this was the time to tell her the truth about himself.

Then she began to talk about herself.

"Bruce and I came here when we were on our honeymoon," she said, which dispelled Jake's thought of holding her hand or putting his arm around her shoulder or turning her to face him and taking her in his arms.

They walked, side by side. He kept his hands in his pockets and walked where the tide had receded to keep from getting his shoes full of sand.

Just as he was thinking he should have taken her elsewhere, she turned her face toward his and spoke to the contrary. "I'm glad we came here tonight, Jake. I never really appreciated the setting. I was so young and so blinded by love. I'm sure you know what that's like."

Jake looked down at the white sand and chuckled. "To a degree," he replied. "But I sort of took all this for granted, having grown up here." He didn't elaborate further. He'd never been blindly in love, where everything faded into the background except the object of one's affection. He stole a glance at Brooke. *And now, am I not a little too old, too mature, for such feelings? Obviously not!*

Brooke shrugged. "I felt that way even in Indiana, without such perfect scenery as this. In one sense it was wonderful, being blindly in love. I can't be like that anymore. In a way, it's a loss, but in another way, it's a gain."

How they got on the topic of love, Jake wasn't sure. But the subject was here and something to be faced realistically. But they were talking about Bruce, were they not? "I suppose human love comes down to what Jesus taught when He said, 'Love your neighbor.' The very vivid lesson is that love is not just a feeling, but love is action."

Brooke nodded. "I expected action to follow and expected the same feelings could never die. There is such a sense of personal failure when marriage doesn't work out."

Brooke told him about her life with Bruce, how she had failed to be the kind of public wife he wanted, and how he had failed to be the homebody she wanted. They weren't suited for each other. They had looked at external appearances and liked what they saw. She had thought his dreams were what she wanted, but after having Ben, her priorities changed. Bruce and his goals were no longer first in her life.

"Maybe it would have been different," she said now, "if I had kept God as the center of my life."

"I know exactly what you mean, Brooke," Jake said. "My life hasn't always been exemplary. In my college days I experimented with just about everything that I shouldn't. I didn't want to be in love, so I played the field, so to speak. It wasn't until I was in my early thirties that I met Meagan when I was working on a summer house for her parents."

As they walked along the beach, Jake told about having believed he was in love with Meagan. They both were going to church, and although he was a Christian, he did not resist the temptation to engage in a physically intimate relationship, justifying it by saying they were only human, consenting adults, planning to spend their lives together.

"Those were only excuses to gratify my own desires," he admitted. He paused, looking over at Brooke. "You don't want to hear this kind of thing," he said.

"I do, Jake," she said softly. "If you want to tell me."

He didn't want to tell her. But he knew it was the only honest thing to do if their relationship was to grow. She put a lot of stock in honesty. After a long sigh, he admitted the relationship was based primarily on the physical. Or maybe it was their concentration on the physical that kept them from getting to know each other fully. "After about two years, the relationship ended."

"You must have loved her very much," Brooke said.

"I suppose I did," he said. "I've learned there are many kinds of love and many degrees. But what I felt for her at the time was what I called love."

He heard the hesitancy in her voice when she looked over at him and asked, "How does that differ from what you call love now?"

Jake wasn't sure how to answer. He knew that so-called puppy love or a crush to a young person could be as real as mature love to an older person. "I suppose it involves all the feelings I had back then, which includes the physical, the selfish, the human aspects. But the kind of love that lasts is not just based on feelings, but on action as well. My actions in my younger days did not fill all the empty spots in my life. Only since I've made God my first priority have I found the peace and purpose that had been missing in my life. I think that love of the right kind must involve the kind of commitment based on biblical principals."

Brooke agreed. "Many times I felt Bruce did not have the kind of commitment to the Lord or to me that he should have had. But I never spoke to him about it. In fact, I tried to gain his approval by trying to be the socialite he wanted." She sighed. "It didn't work. And I knew that God was missing from our lives, but I was as guilty as Bruce of omitting God. Maybe I was more guilty because I knew more about it, having been reared in a Christian home."

"Sometimes," Jake said reflectively, "the worst experiences in our lives are what bring us to our knees before God—where we should have been in the first place."

They walked back toward the boardwalk. This was not a time for taking her in his arms. They were quiet, walking together, as if they were one with the ocean, the sound of the water caressing the shore, the pale moonlight shining on them both.

Taking her in his arms would not satisfy the longing within himself. It would only perpetuate it and perhaps turn his feelings into primarily physical ones. His feelings for Brooke were physical, but he wanted more from her, wanted to give her more. He wanted their relationship to be deep and meaningful and lasting. Taking her in his arms would not convince her of that.

Was this the time to tell her more? Should he stop right now and say, "There's more"? Perhaps his hesitancy was God's way of saying wait. Or perhaps it was his own cowardice. However, the opportune moment passed.

They reached the boardwalk, and the talk turned to the sand on Brooke's feet. He showed her where a knob would bring water out of a small pipe so she could rinse the sand off.

She did so and wiped them on the grass, then slipped into her sandals while holding onto his arm for support.

But he did not take her in his arms for a moonlight kiss. He did not know the touch of her lips, the feel of her body against his, a warm breath against his cheek. He did not know and perhaps that increased his desire for it, intensified his feelings, made their relationship stronger.

He felt she had begun to trust him, just as he'd begun to distrust himself. If he took her in his arms and kissed her, he'd never want to let her go.

"Thank you," Jake said, after they were in the van, heading for Ginger's. "Thank you for making this such a special evening. I'm glad you had dinner with me."

"So am I," she said and glanced over to return his smile.

She still felt the smile in her heart after they picked up Ben, who fell asleep on the second row of seats in the van. When they arrived at the cottage, Jake took him inside, laid him on his bed, and slipped off his tennis shoes and socks.

≈   •

Back in the living room, Jake said what Brooke had already observed.

"I'm real fond of that little boy," he said. "He's fit right in with Ginger's boys."

Brooke nodded. "Ginger's boys take after their momma. They're real easy to relate to." She paused and then added, "And their uncle."

She saw the sudden surprise come into his eyes, followed by a look of pain that was quickly erased by the usual warmth. "Thank you," he said. "And that little boy sleeping in there takes a lot after his mother. You're a good mother, Brooke. I'm impressed."

Emotion welled up in her eyes. She couldn't think of a better compliment. Words like that meant so much more than if he'd said she was pretty or that he liked her hair, or if he'd ogled her as if he liked what he saw. "Thank you, Jake," she said softly. "You couldn't have said anything nicer."

She could have added that his actions toward Ben were

more like a father's than Bruce's had ever been. Bruce had never abused Ben except by omitting the good times they might have had together.

Jake left, after no more contact than gentleness in his eyes and warmth in his voice when he said softly, "Good night, Brooke."

⋆⋆

Later, Brooke lay in bed staring toward the moonlit window, thinking about the evening. She remembered an adage her mother had quoted upon occasion: "One rose does not a summer make."

Brooke added her own interpretation: "One date does not a relationship make."

Just what had been Jake Randolph's intentions? Was he simply being a friend, wanting to ultimately dispel any traces of mistrust she might have of him? Had he suspected she might come to care for him in a special way and wanted to let her know he was still in love with a woman who had rejected him? Had he been trying to tell her she was a fine person, a good mother, and they could be friends? Or was he implying that her spirituality had not matured to the point he wanted in a woman he could be serious about? Was Evelyn more the type of woman a dedicated Christian like him deserved?

Oh, why those doubts?

She closed her eyes against them. Of course she knew. Those years of never being good enough for Bruce had taken their toll.

But what was it Jake had said? Something about our hardest times are when we learn the most. What had she learned? The answer was as close as the question. She'd learned she could make a life for herself and her son without her husband—

without a man. She did not have to depend upon a man for her happiness. Ginger was a wonderful example of that.

Brooke forced the insecurities from her mind, remembering the Scripture about God's love being sufficient. *So, Lord. If Jake Randolph is not for me, I accept that. I can handle that because I have handled losing the love of a husband who meant the world to me. You know what is best for me. I will not struggle with this relationship, but I'm giving it over to You.*

Right before falling into a peaceful sleep, Brooke realized another important thing. She had gone out on a date with a man, had a wonderful time, and related well. That was something she'd thought she'd never be able to do. That was a major accomplishment.

"Thank You, Lord, she breathed as she drifted off into dreamland, feeling certain that everything was resolved within her heart and mind. She could handle whatever the situation.

However, she chided herself the following morning when she remembered her night had been filled with dreams of a couple's walk along the beach beneath a full moon with the sound of mighty ocean waves gently caressing the shore. In her dreams, the man put his arm around the woman and drew her close.

seventeen

Jake knew he didn't need more dinners to determine how he felt about Brooke. A dinner date couldn't possibly tell him any more about her than he knew by seeing her in everyday life relating to her son, caring about a messy, shedding, dirty dog because her son loved him, paying rapt attention to a pastor at church, singing praises to the Lord, relating to people like Ginger and her boys, and planning for her future with determination rather than wallowing in self-pity. He admired her, respected her, and with a feeling of both joy and trepidation he admitted to himself that he loved her. And he loved Ben, that big-eyed, mischievous, exaggerating active little boy who was a part of Brooke.

With the way he felt about Brooke, he couldn't just put his feelings on hold for another two months, maybe not even for two days. They were growing closer. Once Ben started school and Brooke started her nurse's training, it might be easy for them to drift apart. He couldn't chance her growing away from him.

He'd been talking to Brooke about putting up fencing since Taz was growing bigger every day and had already begun to run off around the neighborhood and refuse to come until the mood struck him. Without a fence, they'd soon have to chain him up when Ben played with him outside. Otherwise they would have to keep him in the house.

"I can take you to Bluffton Saturday afternoon to look at fencing," he told Brooke. "While we're there, I'd like for us

136

to stop in, and you can meet my parents."

His heart skipped a beat when she readily accepted the invitation. Maybe after meeting them, she'd see he was from good stock. She would believe him honorable and serious about her.

Surely, by now, she knew he was trustworthy. She'd had a failed marriage and an unfaithful husband. She understood how things could go so wrong without anyone intending for them to, how people could even be blind to it for a while, and the emotional toll it can take. Yes, Brooke was an understanding woman. It was time to tell her about his past.

But he mustn't let her hear it from anyone else. He regretted that he must ask his parents not to mention the past, or at least not the past few years of it. He called his parents. "Mom," he said. "I'd like to stop by tomorrow. I'm bringing Brooke Haddon. I haven't told her about the past yet, so you and Dad just don't bring it up, please."

He listened and heard the inflection in his mom's voice when she asked, sounding like a reprimand, "Jake, if you're serious about this woman, don't you think it would be a good idea to bring everything out into the open?"

"I intend to, Mom. I don't know how serious she is about me, and this is not the kind of thing I go around telling everyone."

"I understand, son," she said. "You have to do what you think is best. I just don't like having to be careful about what I say."

He laughed lightly. She and Ginger were alike in that. They usually spoke their mind. He used to, but he had become more careful in the past few years. "Sorry to put you in this position, Mom."

"Well, Jake. If you're interested in this woman, I definitely want to meet her."

The afternoon sun in a Carolina blue sky spread its warmth on a beautiful day. As they sped along the William Hilton Parkway, heading toward Bluffton, Brooke rolled down the window and felt the air blow her hair. She didn't care if it were mussed. There was such a feeling of freedom. It felt good, sitting beside Jake, feeling the wind on her face and in her hair. This place was perfect for her.

Maybe she had overcome those depressing feelings of guilt, failure, loss, and the fear of raising Ben alone. She'd come to this island feeling washed up. But thanks to Ginger, her boys, and Jake, she had a new lease on life.

Particularly, she owed these feelings to Jake. She'd come to the island feeling she never wanted to be involved with a man again. But Jake had won her trust. He'd shown her what a Christian man should be like. He loved the Lord and tried to live for Him daily.

Also, he'd given her a whole new set of emotions. She'd come here hurt, disappointed, afraid. Jake made her feel like she could conquer the world. Maybe even allow a man in her life again. The past had begun to fade. She'd come to know people whose situations were far worse than hers, and she could count her blessings.

"Penny for your thoughts," Jake said.

Brooke smiled. "You were in them," she said softly.

Jake glanced over, and seeing the reflection of a warm sunny day on her face, he returned the smile, took his hand from the wheel and held hers for a brief moment.

"I hope your parents won't feel like I'm imposing upon them," Brooke said.

"I called and told them I was bringing you. They're looking forward to meeting you," he said, hoping she wouldn't think it too forward of him to make this sound important. Her smile indicated she didn't. "They're just ordinary people," he said.

Bluffton was just across the causeway on the mainland. Jake pointed out homes and a mall he or his dad and their crews had built. Brooke was impressed with his work and the pride he took in it. Apparently, business was good, with Jake being able to buy choice property on Hilton Head.

In no time at all he turned off the main road and drove up a long, curved, tree-lined drive to a lovely, low country home at the end of a cul-de-sac. The wraparound veranda-style front porch lent a gentle southern flavor to the peaceful setting. As soon as they parked, a middle-aged couple who looked to be in their sixties appeared on the porch.

The woman was unmistakably related to Ginger. The family resemblance was evident, and the woman apparently kept herself in shape too. She looked to be the same size as Ginger. Her auburn curls were shorter, and there was some gray sprinkled in. The man was tall like Jake and maybe twenty pounds heavier. His hair was darker and thinner than Jake's. There was a family resemblance there, too, and he must have been as handsome as Jake when he was younger.

Todd Randolph shook her hand, and Cora hugged her after Jake made the introductions. Brooke was reminded that she'd heard somewhere that southern folks had a monopoly on hugs and hospitality. This couple seemed to prove that.

She liked the interior of the house, too, from the moment she walked in and saw the cathedral ceiling, hardwood floor, and cozy fireplace. It wasn't as elegant as the home she and Bruce had owned in Indiana, but it was more plush than her parents' modest home. This one was very nice, as inviting as its owners. Cora took them directly to the large eat-in kitchen.

"She always has cookies," Jake said, with a grin. "Made from scratch."

"And you've never been too old for them either," his mother said mockingly. They all laughed at that as Jake dug into the cookie jar and passed it to Brooke, who chose a big chunk full of chocolate chips.

Todd and Cora each helped themselves to a cookie too. "Come outside," Cora said, "and see where we live most of the time."

When they stepped outside, Brooke could understand why they would spend time out back. A lovely blue-bottomed pool sparkled in the sunlight, surrounded by white concrete and a low white railing. Beyond that was a tennis court. The rest of the spacious lawn was like green velvet, dotted with oaks and tall palmettos, and farther back stood a huge magnolia tree.

"Have a seat," Todd Randolph said, gesturing to the chairs beneath the awning over the white tabby patio, flanked by azalea hedges that had lost their spring blossoms several weeks ago and now boasted summer's lush green leaves.

Brooke had to look closely to see that a chain-link fence surrounded the property, for she could look out through the trees at a spectacular view of a lagoon.

"This is lovely," Brooke said.

"Thank you," Cora said. "Todd built it for us several years ago. I guess you know Ginger and Jake live in our old home place."

Brooke nodded, realizing that either Ginger or Jake must have talked to them about her.

Cora and Todd talked about having grown up on Hilton Head. Todd's dad had been an architect and had helped design many of the structures on the island. "I remember the day they turned on the electricity on Hilton Head," Todd said.

"It was in 1951," Cora said, finishing his sentence.

Todd nodded. "Then the building began. That was one of the most lucrative jobs to have."

"We liked Hilton Head," Cora added. "But after Todd had his heart surgery and he sold the business to Jake and—"

Coughing, she broke off her sentence, and Brooke detected a strange tension in the air. Brooke wondered what Cora had been about to say but didn't. Perhaps she was mistaken, or maybe it was simply difficult for Cora to talk about her husband's surgery.

"Anyway," Todd said after what seemed to be a strained moment of silence, "we always talked about traveling after I retired, doing things together. I was always too busy. She was busy too, teaching those little kids in the second grade. I'd seen men younger than me end up gravely ill and then dying, so I decided that since I'd had surgery, it might be now or never that we saw the world. I could leave the business in good hands. And I did," he said. "The best."

Brooke smiled, seeing the obvious love and pride in Todd's eyes when he looked at Jake. Then Cora was saying, "Well, tell us about you, Brooke."

What could she say? "I'm from Indiana. I had two years of nurses' training and got married and had a little boy, who's now five. Over a year ago, my husband was killed in an auto accident. His parents gave me the cottage on Hilton Head that Jake's been making repairs on. Let's see," she said, wondering what else to say. "I'm planning to resume nurses' training after Ben starts to school." She thought a moment. "Oh, and I have a dog."

They laughed as she and Jake talked about some of Taz's experiences, especially being a "miniature" who now weighed about twenty-five pounds.

"You two apparently play tennis," Brooke said, looking toward the court.

"Play?" Jake scoffed. "I don't think Ginger and I ever beat these two."

"Now, there was one time," Todd said playfully, and they all laughed. Then he looked at Brooke. "I guess you know the island's famous for its golf and tennis courts. The best women pros in the world come here to play in the Family Circle Cup every year."

Brooke had known about the golf but hadn't realized that the island was so famous for tennis until the older couple clued her in.

"We could have a game right now," Todd said, standing, ready to get the rackets and balls.

Brooke couldn't help but laugh at his enthusiasm and his challenge. "Maybe another time," she said and blushed to think she assumed there would be another time. "I haven't played tennis since I was in high school."

He sat down again. "Promise! Another time."

Jake explained that they wanted to go to the home improvement store.

"And I need to get back," Brooke added. "Ben's complained about his tummy hurting the past couple of days. He might be coming down with something, so I'd better get him to bed early."

"I like them very much," Brooke could honestly say, after she and Jake were on the road.

Jake nodded and told her that his dad had built up Randolph Construction Company into a lucrative business. At a very early age Jake had wielded a hammer and saw. He'd worked for his dad for wages during high school and college, when school was out for the summer.

"I went to college on a football scholarship, and I majored in architecture and design, thinking I might become an engineer." He shook his head. "But that wasn't for me. I'm an outdoor person. I love the manual work and decided to work for Dad. Then, like he said, he retired and sold me the business."

Brooke felt that strange tension again. And again, maybe she was mistaken. His easy flow of conversation stopped only because he was turning into the parking lot in front of the home improvement store.

꙳

Jake could tell his parents took to Brooke and liked her immediately. They didn't have to say it. He saw it in the way they talked to her and in how his Dad found a way to ask her to come back again. He saw it in the way they both looked at him and grinned like he'd won the lottery right before he and Brooke left.

But however much he wanted it, he didn't have to have his parents' approval. He was a grown man who wanted Brooke's approval. He was happy to have her sitting beside him in the truck as if they belonged together. It seemed natural when they walked down the long aisle and she started to turn in one direction and he in another and he reached for her hand.

"This way," he said. He kept holding her hand, and she didn't try to remove it. *I want her by my side,* he thought, *always.* Surely, God wouldn't have brought her into his life and given him this love for her if it wasn't right. Yes, he would have to talk to her this very night.

He was still holding her hand when it happened. He stopped dead in his tracks and stood like a statue. The couple directly in front of them did the same.

He stood eye-to-eye, face-to-face with Meagan.

eighteen

Brooke felt Jake's hand tighten on hers before he let go. His arms were down at his side as if he were standing at attention. She looked at the man and dark-eyed woman, straight ahead, staring at them.

After what seemed an incredible eternity, Jake spoke. The man mumbled a half-hearted greeting, the woman stared wide-eyed as if seeing a ghost, and then both hurried away, pretending to be interested in something in the store. Brooke saw a muscle in the side of Jake's jaw continue to jerk. His face was flushed. He turned to look at the fencing as if it were his enemy.

After a moment, he shook his head. "I'm sorry. I was surprised. I know that couple, and it would have been pointless to try and introduce you."

"Don't worry about it," Brooke said, sorry for the broken camaraderie that had vanished between her and Jake. She glanced over her shoulder and saw, way up the aisle, that the woman, whose black hair was pulled back into a bun, did the same. Turning back quickly, Brooke tried to focus on fencing.

She heard herself talking unnaturally fast. "Maybe chain-link would be best. I can see that Ginger wants wood since she needs privacy to teach her aerobics class. But I liked the effect of your parents' back yard, and since I have close neighbors it might be best to have a see-through fence.

"Sounds like a good idea," Jake agreed. "Ben and Taz

would probably be happier with that too. If this is what you want, I can measure and see how much you need."

As they walked back through the store, Jake didn't hold her hand. He hadn't been his pleasant, natural self since seeing the couple. Brooke didn't know if she had a right to ask, but she and Jake were becoming closer. She wanted to know.

"Who was the couple?" she asked when they returned to the truck.

He didn't have to ask which couple.

Jake sighed heavily, traveled slowly down the street, and turned a corner before answering. "That was Meagan," he said, which was no surprise to Brooke. After a pause he added, "The man was Oswald Jenkins. He used to work for Dad and me. There was a time when I asked him, as a friend, to watch out for her while I had to be away." Jake paused. "He did. They're married now."

When he didn't add anything else, Brooke said, "There seemed to be lot of tension there in the store. Are you. . .still in love with her, Jake?"

"You're right, there was tension," he said. "But not for the reasons you think. I have to talk to you about all this."

Brooke waited, but he didn't say anything more. His mood had changed. Looking ahead, she noticed a cloud had appeared on the horizon. Was that a symbol of what was to happen? She could understand if Jake were still in love. But he denied it. Was he living with regrets, as she had done so long about Bruce? Why wouldn't he confide in her? Communication was so important.

"If you want to talk to me, Jake, I'm willing to listen," she offered.

At the same time, rain began to pelt the windshield. She rolled up her window and watched the dark clouds blow across the sky and the treetops bend with the wind.

Jake rolled up his window and switched on the windshield wipers. They reminded Brooke of giant fingers shaking back and forth as if she should have known better than allow her heart to become vulnerable.

"There is something I should tell you, Brooke," Jake said, keeping his attention on the cloudburst striking the truck and the road. "I haven't known when the time is right. But I need enough time to explain things to you."

"You don't have to explain anything to me, Jake," she told him.

"Yes, I do, Brooke. Because of what you've come to mean to me. I owe it to you."

During the rest of the drive to Ginger's and then to her cottage, Jake was unusually quiet except for a few comments to Ben. His mind was obviously elsewhere.

Or, Brooke asked herself, *is it his heart that is elsewhere?*

❧

Long into the night, Brooke thought about Jake's words and his mood after seeing Meagan. He indicated there was something ominous he had to tell her. She felt she could take it or accept whatever he might tell her. Jake had already revealed that he'd had a physical relationship with Meagan. But if the Lord had forgiven him, then who was she not to do so?

It couldn't be as bad as he made it seem. Whatever the situation, it was probably magnified in his mind since he was so intent upon making a good impression and being a Christian example. She could understand that, remembering how she felt that all eyes were upon her, judging her, knowing she was living a lie when her marriage was failing. Being out of God's will and the guilt that brought when you knew better placed a heavy burden on a person.

Another thought struck her. Perhaps he had an incurable disease. Could that be a reason why, at his age, he wasn't married or seeing anyone? But he was obviously perfectly healthy. And if he were dying, he wouldn't be taking her out and saying he cared for her, would he?

Brooke rolled over and punched the pillow, getting into her usual comfortable sleeping position on her stomach. She mustn't spend the night trying to figure out what she couldn't possibly know. She knew Jake. She pushed aside the thought, *But you thought you knew Bruce.*

Finally she drifted off to sleep, praying that God would give Jake the courage to reveal whatever he wanted to reveal to her and give her the grace to accept it in a Christlike manner.

❧

Morning came too soon. She hadn't slept enough. During breakfast she noticed the spot on the ceiling was bigger and browner. Ben wasn't feeling too well either. But her mind was set on hearing Jake out and getting this behind them. During Sunday school, Jake seemed to be his usual jovial self, talking, laughing, greeting, discussing, but Brooke had come to know him well enough to realize all that was colored with a touch of reserve. She knew he was afraid of what he had to say to her.

After church, she expected it, when they all walked to the parking lot together and Jake asked if she'd stay while he talked with her. Ginger said she'd take Ben home with her. She'd save lunch for Brooke and Jake.

Was it going to take that long?

Jake led her out to the privacy of the sunken prayer garden where they walked down the steps to a bench beneath a live oak. All signs of the storm last night had vanished in the bright sunshine of the morning. While the crowds exited the front of the sanctuary, a short distance away from the garden, Brooke walked around and touched what was likely one of the last remaining blossoms of a bygone spring.

When the sound of dispersing crowds faded, Brooke turned to see that Jake sat, leaning forward with his forearms on his thighs, his hands clasped, his head bent, and his eyes closed.

He straightened when she sat beside him, ready for whatever confession he wanted to make to her. She smiled encouragingly. After all, she'd heard that confession was good for the soul.

She was ready. Or at least she thought she was ready when Jake turned and took her hands in his. But never in a million years did she expect to hear what Jake had to say.

"I'm an ex-con, Brooke. I've spent time in federal prison. And I'm still on probation."

It didn't really register for what seemed an eternity. Slowly, slowly it dawned. An ex-con had associated with her child. An ex-con had come into her home, under false pretenses, had spoken beautiful words of love—for God, for her, for her son, for her dog.

Jake Randolph was a con-man. Like Bruce. Just like Bruce. It all came flooding in on her—feelings and emotions she thought she'd dealt with. But here she was, duped again! Her distrust of men was again confirmed.

She could be thankful for one thing. That wall of reserve had thawed but hadn't completely melted from around her heart. Hadn't she expected to be disappointed again?

But could this be a nightmare? Was Jake really a. . .a crook?

And had his crime been so bad he even feared telling her about it?

She had to get away from this. From him.

❧

The instant he spoke, Jake knew he'd blurted out the news too quickly. He should have led up to it with an explanation. With sinking heart, he watched the color drain from Brooke's face. He saw the smile fade. He watched her eyes stare in horror. Her expression was what he had feared. She looked just like Meagan when he'd told her he'd been arrested, and why. Meagan wanted nothing more to do with him. Meagan hadn't even stayed around for an explanation.

And now, Brooke was going to leave too. As if in slow motion, she moved her hands out of his. She was going to bolt!

"Brooke," he said, the same as he had said to Meagan. "I wasn't guilty."

A tinge of color appeared in her cheeks. She was shaking her head. She stood, still staring at him, unable to get any words out.

He repeated, "Brooke. I wasn't guilty."

He'd thought she was about to faint and reached out for her, but she shrugged him away. Just then, the associate pastor called his name.

"Jake," he summoned. "Your sister called and said for you and Brooke to come home immediately. She said it was urgent."

❧

If Jake had tried to talk to her on the way to Ginger's, Brooke wouldn't have acknowledged it. Something terrible must have happened. *Was it Ben?* She should have been with her son. *Oh, Lord. Please, please, let everything be all right.* But if everything were all right, Ginger wouldn't have called.

When Jake screeched to a halt in front of Ginger's house, a neighbor and the three boys ran out the front door and met them at the truck. *Where is Ben? He isn't there! Something terrible has happened!*

The boys looked scared to death, pale as ghosts, and the look on the neighbor lady's face indicated something dreadful had happened. Did he fall into the pool, unnoticed? Had he run out into the road and been hit by a car? Had he fallen off the swing set and hurt himself? What had happened? "Ben? Is Ben okay?"

"Ginger drove him to the hospital," the neighbor said. "I don't know what all happened. She had Mike call me."

"His stomach hurt," Mike said.

"And he threw up," George added, while the frightened little boys nodded their agreement. Danny's lips quivered, and he started to sob. The neighbor pulled him to her and put her arms around him.

"The medical center?" Jake asked.

"Yes," the neighbor lady said. "That's where she said she'd take him."

Appendicitis! was flashing through Brooke's mind like a red danger signal. She had enough nurses' training to know what the symptoms were. Thinking back, she could see other signs. He hadn't eaten much at all yesterday, saying he wasn't very hungry. He'd had problems with constipation, but she had accredited that to his not having eaten right.

Maybe it was just a virus, she tried telling herself. But in her heart she knew better. Appendicitis was fairly common; however, if the appendix ruptured, it could turn into peritonitis. And that was much too serious for a little guy like Ben.

"Hurry," she whispered.

"Yes," Jake said, not taking his eyes from the road speeding past them.

Brooke felt as if her entire being was one desperate prayer. *Oh God, he's so little, so young, and I'm not with him.*

nineteen

Ginger was waiting at the emergency room door when Brooke arrived. "His stomachache got worse, and his temperature sky-rocketed," she explained. "He threw up, and I got him here as fast as I could."

"Thanks," Brooke said hastily and rushed over to the desk. Ginger and Jake were right behind her.

The receptionist wanted all sorts of information, but Brooke wanted to see her son. Finally a nurse came out to talk to her. "He's just fine. They're running tests and trying to bring his fever down. You'll be able to see him in just a few minutes."

Brooke nodded and relented to answering the receptionist's questions, the most pertinent being, "Who is your insurance company?"

The receptionist looked like Brooke felt when she replied, "I don't have insurance."

"Come sit down," Ginger said, taking Brooke by the shoulders. Feeling numb, Brooke followed her lead to a corner of the waiting room.

Brooke was about to say no to any suggestion like coffee or food when Jake started speaking, but his words weren't what she expected to hear. "Let's sit down and pray about this, Brooke," he said softly.

Yes, she wanted that. This was not a time to think of anything but her son.

They sat. He took her hands, bowed his head, and presented

little Ben to the Lord. He lifted the young boy up and told God what had happened, as if God didn't know.

"Thank You for blessing Brooke with Ben for over five years," he prayed. "Lord, we know everything is Yours and in Your hands. We're placing our faith and trust in You, that this situation will be controlled only by You. Be with the doctors, the nurses, all the workers here, and with Brooke— that she may feel the comfort of Your presence. Thy will be done. In Jesus' name, amen."

Brooke felt it. The fear, the urge not to say, "Thy will be done," but to beg God to save Ben's life. She tried to move away, but Jake wouldn't let go of her tension-filled hands. "Lord, I have no strength," she finally began. "I know You love him more than I am capable of loving. But I want him with me, and I pray You may see fit to allow that. Thank You for the years of joy I've experienced with Ben. He was my life jacket in my sea of trouble. Lord, help me to be his life jacket now that he is in trouble. I pray that Ben's needs will be met by You—and I want his recovery—but Lord, I'm trying to want Your will."

She wasn't even sure she could mean it wholeheartedly, but knew what she must pray. "Thy. . .will. . .be. . .done," came out in a choked whisper. "I'm trusting You, Lord. Forgive me for thinking of myself. Help me to be what Ben needs at this time."

She began to sob, and feeling Brooke's hands relax, Jake released them. "Let me hold you," he said. She allowed him to come closer and hold her head against his shoulder. With the strength of his arms around her, she cried. When she felt cried out, she thanked him, then went to the restroom to splash cold water on her face.

Ginger had stayed, but Jake was gone when Brooke

returned to the waiting room. She felt empty without him there. At the same time she felt a great calm, rather like a cloud of comfort, had surrounded her, keeping her from fear and wondering and pleading. She felt covered by a blanket of God's presence and love.

Finally, the doctor talked with her. "All tests indicate appendicitis," he said, confirming her suspicions. He related that they'd performed an abdominal sonography and a blood test and that there was increased pain on the right side of Ben's abdomen. "There seems to be a slight perforation of the intestines, and we suspect an abscess," the doctor said. "We will monitor him closely for a few hours and give him antibiotic therapy to reduce any infection. That has to be done before we can consider surgery."

"Suppose it. . .ruptures?" Brooke asked, knowing that such an event could put her son in grave danger.

The doctor spoke confidently. "We are prepared for emergencies," he replied.

Shortly, a nurse came to say Brooke could go to Ben's room. She held his hot little hand. She talked to him and told him that she loved him. She told him that God loved him and His Spirit would not leave him for a moment. She prayed aloud for his recovery.

He was a brave little tyke, but Brooke saw the concern in his feverish eyes. Soon, he closed them and fell asleep.

"He's so sick," Brooke said when she returned to Ginger in the waiting room.

"I'm so sorry," Ginger said.

"It's no one's fault," Brooke said. "He had symptoms, but I didn't put them all together. I'm just grateful you got him to the hospital."

"I was scared to death," she said and quickly rose and

walked over to the window. Brooke saw her shoulders shaking and knew she was crying.

Brooke went over to her and they embraced.

Ginger sniffed. "I should be helping you, not the other way around."

"You are," Brooke said. "But why don't you go home? Your boys need you."

"Jake's coming back in a little while. I'll go then."

Brooke didn't have strength enough to argue. She refused to allow anything into her mind but Ben. He was her responsibility. Yet, after Jake returned, his presence helped. She could call her parents and have them fly down, but somehow Jake's optimistic outlook was a comfort. He was someone she had come to count on during the past months. She would not send him away.

❧

Hours later, Ben was taken into surgery. Brooke would not consider going home. Jake didn't even suggest it. She told him he could.

"I know that," he said. "But I'm not going to."

She bit on her lip to keep from bawling again.

"I don't want to cause you any distress," he said. "I want to be here for Ben and for you if you need me. There are no strings attached."

He didn't ask her to have a cup of coffee or listen to him. He wasn't trying to persuade her about anything. He just said, "I left to talk to the pastor. There are now around-the-clock prayer meetings going on for you and Ben. Ginger will take care of Taz."

When the flood again ran down her face, he got up, and she wondered if he was going to hold her again. If he tried, she would let him.

Instead, he said, "I'll be back," and walked out of the room.

Later he returned with a toy dog that looked a lot like Taz and had a red balloon tied to its collar.

He sat down with it. "For when he wakes up," he said.

✿

After surgery, the doctor came into the waiting room, all smiles. Brooke breathed a sigh of relief when he said that surgery revealed that peritonitis had not developed and that there was no infection. Ben would have a scar about one and a half inches long.

"Oh, thank you," she said.

The doctor nodded. "You'll be notified as soon as he's out of recovery and into his own room."

Brooke turned to Jake who held out his hands. She took them and they closed their eyes. "Thank You, God," Jake prayed.

"Thank You," Brooke added.

✿

"I like this one," Ben said to Jake when he gave him the stuffed dog. "But I want Taz to come and see me."

"No way," Jake said. "That monster would eat all your Jell-O and crackers."

Ben smirked. "I want pizza anyway."

"A few more days and you'll have your pizza. Now you rest, so you can get well and go home. If you're good, I'll smuggle a few boys in here to see you."

"Yeah!" Ben said and flopped his head over, pretending to go to sleep.

Brooke was full of gratitude to the Lord for Ben's successful surgery and recovery and that Jake popped in to cheer him up. When he wasn't in Ben's room, she noticed him in other children's rooms, talking, joking, and he always prayed with them before leaving.

He might be a former criminal, but didn't Jesus say you would know what people are like by their fruits? *What are Jake's fruits?* she asked herself and could readily answer. *He helps other people. He is caring. He does good works. He serves others. He has that water-basin attitude that Jesus admonished His followers to have.*

And what are my fruits? she questioned and knew they were not nearly as obvious as Jake's. *I, too, have made mistakes. I didn't put God and His will and ways first in my life during my marriage. Maybe if I had been a dedicated Christian, I could have helped Bruce. Maybe God gave me to Bruce for that reason, and maybe I failed. I never said that I didn't want the big house, the fine car, the beautiful clothes, the attention. I did want them. And is that any different from Jake's wanting something so much he committed a criminal act to get it?*

But Jake had said he wasn't guilty.

Had she, with her judgmental attitude, condemned an innocent man?

She looked up from where she sat beside Ben's bed while he slept. Jake stood in the doorway. Seeing that Ben was asleep, he motioned her outside.

"Brooke, I heard you say you don't have insurance. I can help you—"

She shook her head before he could finish. "I appreciate that, Jake. But I have to try and do this on my own. If I'm going to have faith in God, then I have to depend on Him, not other people."

"But sometimes His way of working is through other people," Jake said.

"I know, but I have to try. Can you sit with Ben for a while?"

"Sure," he said, looking as if she had offered him the world.

&

Brooke did the only thing she could. She withdrew her money out of savings and deposited it in her checking account. That was the money she'd put aside for her nurses' training and for her and Ben to live on.

But she had no choice. The hospital bill had to be paid.

There were only a few weeks until Ben would start to school. Maybe she could scrimp some way, then find some kind of job to see them through. Without skills, she had no idea what kind of job she could get.

When Brooke returned to pay the bill, the secretary told her the amount.

"Are you sure?" she asked.

"Pretty sure I'm sure," the woman answered. "You don't think it's right?"

"I thought it was more."

"Oh, the check we got paid part of it."

"Check?" Brooke questioned. "What check?"

"Let's see." She fumbled around on her desk. "This one," she said. "It hasn't been deposited yet."

Brooke stared, hardly able to believe it. A sizeable check that would pay a big chunk of the bill was from the church. "Who gave this to you?" she asked.

"The pastor," the woman replied. "He's here all the time to see patients." She smiled broadly. "This happens quite often."

Brooke could hardly see to write her own check. This wasn't going to take her last penny after all. *Oh, God.*

Forgive my little faith. I'll try to do better.

When Ginger came later and Brooke told her about the church's gift, Ginger was not surprised. "Our church is a giving church," she said. "They do this kind of thing."

"I'll bet Jake was in on it," Brooke said.

Ginger grinned. "I think it's all confidential."

Brooke nodded. "Want to get a bite of supper with me?"

"It's about time you ate."

Brooke knew it was also about time she mentioned the situation between her and Jake. "He told me he was in prison, Ginger. That knocked me for a loop. I feel like I went into shock."

"Didn't he tell you he wasn't guilty?"

"Right before the associate pastor said you called," Brooke replied. "Since then, all I've thought about was Ben. But when Jake said he wasn't guilty, something flashed through my mind. It was a movie I saw. A prisoner was asked what he was in for. He quipped that nobody in that place was guilty, and everyone laughed, indicating they all were guilty."

"I saw a movie like that," Ginger replied bluntly. "And it seems to me the one who said that was really innocent."

Feeling reprimanded, Brooke admitted, "I don't even know what Jake's crime was."

Ginger's eyebrows lifted and she said blandly, "Income tax evasion,"

"Oh!" Brooke exclaimed. Her reaction was one of relief. Before that moment, she didn't realize that all sorts of suspicions had lurked in her mind—perversion, drugs, illegal schemes. Strangely she felt laughter about to bubble up in her throat. It wasn't funny. It was criminal.

Ginger laughed and exclaimed impishly, "Wouldn't we all like to evade that!"

"Yes," Brooke agreed. "But we don't."

Ginger silently picked at her food.

Finally, Brooke said, "Jake said he didn't do it. I shouldn't question."

"Yes, you should, Brooke," Ginger said, looking up. "And I understand. It's so hard to trust anyone again after your heart has been trampled by a man. But if you want to know Jake's story, I think you should hear it from him. I'm the sister of the accused man, and I believe in Jake. You have to find it in your own heart to believe Jake or not—to trust him or not. And if you think he was guilty, you have to look at what kind of life Jake lives now."

twenty

Brooke had been taking a look at the kind of life Jake lived for months. When he came to the hospital that night, she apologized for having doubted him.

"I don't blame you," he said. "I blurted out the fact but didn't tell you the story behind it. I'd like to tell you, if you want to hear it."

Brooke listened intently while Jake talked far into the night, leaving out nothing, blaming himself where he was wrong.

"You remember I told you that it might seem cruel or restrictive to keep Taz on a leash while training him?" Jake asked, and Brooke nodded. "Well, I feel like God had me on a leash in prison, but His instruction has been the best in my life. Before that, I was a believer. I never doubted there was a God, and I believed He was the God of the Bible. I never doubted that Jesus was His Son and that He died on the cross for the sins of the world.

"However, it wasn't really personal for me. Oh, I prayed when something went wrong. But it was always a "gimme" type of prayer. I never had the Spirit of God leading me. I never felt the obligation to tell others that Jesus truly changes a life. That He gives peace, calm, hope, purpose, meaning."

Brooke felt as if his words echoed so much of the belief that had been in her mind for most of her life, but hadn't always been in her heart. She was so grateful that since coming to this island, meeting Jake and Ginger, getting involved in the church, she knew the difference.

"I learned that I was not in control of my life, that I needed to depend solely on the Lord. I was in a situation not of my making, and no one was able to help me," Jake said. "Not family, friends, attorneys—no one. No matter what, some people will always believe I'm guilty." His moment of sadness quickly turned to joy. "I didn't commit that sin, but I have committed others, and I needed the blood of Jesus to wash me clean. Those six months in prison became a time when I searched the Word of God, made it a lamp unto my feet, a light unto my path."

"Oh, Jake," Brooke said sincerely. "Even if you had committed that crime, I know the kind of man you are today. I've never known a person who lived his Christianity more devotedly than you."

Jake had to force back the realization that, although she complimented him, it sounded like she might still have a little doubt about his innocence. "Even if you had committed the crime," she had said. But he would try and dwell on the positive side of her words.

"Brooke," he said. "I love you. I would like to marry you and take care of you and Ben for the rest of your lives."

When she hesitated, rather than make her too uncomfortable, he added, "And Taz?"

She laughed lightly. "Oh, Jake. That's so tempting. But that's the very reason I can't consider anything like that right now. I have a money problem. I have a son to support. I was helpless after Bruce died. I need to be able to stand on my own two feet and support my son without having to depend on a man or on my parents. I think I owe that to myself and to Ben." Seeing his nod, despite the disappointment in his eyes, she added, "And Taz."

He laughed then, briefly, then said seriously, "I admire you for that, Brooke. I won't pressure you. But I'll be here, when you're ready."

❧

The next morning, Jake loaded the van with the toys, flowers, balloons, and cards Ben had received in the hospital and then drove Brooke and Ben home. Ginger and the boys were waiting with lunch ready when they arrived.

Brooke didn't have to cook for a week, with all the food church people brought. The neighbors came, even the young couple who had kept to themselves and had rarely said more than "hello" before.

The visitor who offered the most interesting information, however, was Evelyn, who came one evening while Jake was painting the kitchen ceiling. He'd climbed into the attic portion and found a hole at the very tip of the roof and plugged it.

Evelyn brought a card signed by the children in Ben's Sunday school class. "You're so blessed to have a man like Jake looking after you two," she said when Brooke walked her to the door. "Makes me pine away for my guy. He's in the military, so we can only communicate through the mail or by telephone."

Brooke felt guilty about having ever felt jealous of Evelyn. She realized what she'd missed, too, by not being part of a church family for so many years. People who didn't go to church just didn't realize what they were missing in the way of love and fellowship.

And yes, she was blessed. Jake was true to his word about not pressuring her, but he was there for her and Ben. He fenced in the back yard and built a dog house. Ben helped him paint the dog house—and the grass!

But Brooke was delighted that Ben was learning to use his

hands, not just for a friendly handshake, but for something more constructive.

"Come look, Mom," Ben called, and she went outside to compliment them rather than just peek out the kitchen window. "Miss Evelyn said Jesus was a cartpender," Ben said, his big eyes shining.

"She's right," Jake said.

"Well, I'm gonna grow up and be a cartpender just like Jake and Jesus."

"That's a very worthy goal, darling," Brooke said, looking at Jake's surprised but pleased expression.

❧

Many times, Brooke thought of how much easier things would be if she married Jake instead of finding a way to support herself and Ben. But if God wanted her to be a nurse, He would work that out. Fall was on the way, and she had to make her moves. She and Ginger enrolled their boys in kindergarten and were assured Ben and Danny could be in the same class.

Deciding to check out the cost of nurses' training, Brooke asked Ginger to keep Ben while she went to the university to talk to an advisor. When the advisor said she couldn't get the lower in-state tuition, Brooke knew her hopes were dashed. She couldn't afford the tuition, keep the house running, find time to work, and still spend time with Ben and have time to study. It seemed impossible, and she said as much.

The advisor pushed his dark-rimmed glasses farther up his nose and smiled. "There's a nearby hospital with a plan that might suit you," he said, peering through his lenses to find a folder in his filing cabinet. "Here it is." He returned to his seat. "The hospital will pay tuition if the student commits to work at the hospital after completing the training. Of course, if the individual decides not to work at the hospital, then that student is obligated to repay the hospital."

Brooke bit on her lip and fought back tears of relief. Her eyes automatically lifted to the ceiling, toward heaven. It was as if she could see that bright shining path of Easter morning and she was walking on it toward a clear blue sky. *I didn't even have faith things would work out this way. But I prayed. Oh, God, forgive my lack of faith. I'll try to do better.*

After checking with the hospital to confirm the possibility, she rushed back to tell Ginger. "Most of the money I had saved was for tuition," she said excitedly. "But I'm not going to have to pay tuition. I can't believe this. I don't have a lot, but I'm better off now, even with having paid Ben's hospital bill, than I was when I thought I was going to have to pay tuition."

Ginger just grinned knowingly. "The Lord works in mysterious ways."

"Yeah," Brooke agreed, and they offered a prayer of thanks.

"Where's Jake?" Brooke asked, thinking he should be off work and hoping he hadn't gone to her house needlessly.

"Not far from here," Ginger said. "He met this older couple when Ben was in the hospital. Grandparents of a child who was in for a concussion he got from falling off his bike. He wasn't wearing a helmet. The grandpa had bypass surgery three months before. Jake found out they could use some help, so he's been over there a few times."

"I wonder," Brooke said, "if he could use a partner."

Ginger scratched her auburn curls, looking dumbfounded. Suddenly realization dawned. "By all means, go ask!" She gave directions to their house.

Brooke stopped by a bakery for rolls, then drove up to the house. The woman answered the door. "I understand Jake

Randolph is here making repairs," Brooke said. The woman confirmed it and graciously invited her in, led her to the kitchen, and introduced her to her husband, who was talking to Jake while he worked.

Jake appeared shocked as Brooke gave the rolls to the woman. "I'm from a church up the way," she said. "I heard your husband recently got out of the hospital, and I wondered if there's anything I can do."

"Why, how sweet," the woman gushed, and Brooke knew she was feeling overwhelmed, the way Brooke had felt when Ginger had come to her house. "But no, I don't think we need anything. We're doing fine." She laughed and spoke ironically, saying they had trouble keeping up with her husband's medicine. "He has so much to take and forgets it half the time. When I try to help, I have no idea if he took it or not."

Soon, Brooke and the woman were sitting at the kitchen table, and Brooke made out a schedule for the medicine. She made two copies. "I'll have copies run off of this, and he or you can check it off each time he takes a pill. If the doctor changes the dosage, just make the change on every copy. But he must check it off when he takes each pill."

"I'll see to that. Oh, you're a dear."

Jake packed up his tool box, and Brooke made it a point to leave at the same time as he.

Outside, walking toward their vehicles, Jake asked, "What was that all about?"

She lifted her chin saucily, "You're not the only person in the world with a water-basin mentality, Jake Randolph. You've been a wonderful example to me of Christian service, and I intend to make it a part of my lifestyle too."

He grinned. "You're a girl after my own heart."

"You're absolutely right," she replied.

Before her meaning could register, she jumped into her car and sped away.

By the time she got home with Ben, and he ran out back with Taz, Jake was on her doorstep. He stood there, holding onto the post, one foot on the step and the other on the porch. "What did you mean by that remark?"

Brooke backed up against the banister near him, on the other side of the post. She related how God had worked out her financial situation. "I can go to school without having to get another job. I can still be here for Ben and have time to study. So you see, I don't have to find a man to support me."

Jake realized he was nodding a little too vigorously and knew his smile was pasted on. Yes, it looked like Brooke had moved on. She didn't need him or any man. And that's how it should be. That's what he'd tried so hard to instill in Ginger. It had been a long hard climb, but Ginger had come to realize that, and now Ginger had influenced Brooke. *So I'm partially responsible for this*, he thought with a sense of both pride and disappointment.

"I don't have to have a man," she reiterated, "but I want one."

"You. . .you do?" His eyes met hers.

Brooke nodded. "I do. But there are certain requirements."

"Like. . . ?"

"Well, first of all he has to have a water-basin mentality."

Jake drew in a breath. He dared not hope she was saying what she seemed to be indicating, but there was definitely a look of mischief in her eyes. "You, um, have anyone in mind?" he asked.

"Yeah. He's handsome, strong, giving, loving—"

"Then I should leave," he said, turning as if to go.

"Oh, no," she said, reaching out to grab his arm. "That man is you, Jake Randolph. You said you loved me. If you have changed your mind. . ."

"Yes, I have," he said immediately, and Brooke jerked back like she was shot. Then he smiled that wonderful smile, and his eyes gleamed with such affection that she wasn't sure she could take it. "I changed my mind every minute of every day. I kept saying, 'Jake, you're not going to pine away your life thinking about a woman who doesn't love you. You're not going to waste another minute.' So you see, I changed my mind all day and all night long. But my heart never changed."

His hands were on her shoulders. "I love you, Brooke. I would like for us to spend the rest of our lives together." Exasperated, he shook his head. "I didn't mean to propose or anything."

"Then just what are you suggesting?"

"Brooke, you're deliberately putting me on the spot."

"Yes," she said. "I'm afraid to believe what we might be saying."

"Let's just be honest," he said.

"I love you, Jake," she said.

He reached into his pocket, and her heart beat faster, wondering if he'd been carrying around a ring. It wasn't a ring. It was a newspaper clipping. "I want you to read this, Brooke. It might help you find peace about my past and let you know that I was telling the truth."

"No." She pushed his hand away. "I believe you, Jake. I trust you."

He ignored her words. "I didn't want you to read this until you decided within your own heart what kind of guy I am. You needed to trust me on your own, Brooke, and not because I proved it."

"I'm sorry," she said.

"No, don't be. Now that you trust me, I want you to read this."

Brooke took the clipping. The headline read "Martin Gage Commits Suicide." The article was all about Jake's partner, who had left a suicide note admitting that he alone was guilty and explaining that he had not been able to quit his gambling and he had lost everything—his self respect, his wife and children, his home. He asked that Jake and others in the community forgive him.

"Oh, Jake."

"I feel sorry for him," he said. "But don't feel sorry for me. I was convicted of the same crime as Martin Gage because I was a partner and should have known what was going on. That was evidence enough to convict me. Then, when I was in prison, a pastor came and asked a group of us, 'If you were accused of being a Christian, would there be enough evidence to convict you?' My honest answer was no. I decided then and there that my life would be different. For the rest of my life I want there to be enough evidence to convict me of being a follower of Jesus."

"Jake," Brooke said, moving closer to him. "When I came here, I thought it would take years before I could even consider having a man in my life. You've changed my mind and my life. But," she asked, "how would you feel about your wife going to school and working as a nurse?"

"Proud," he said immediately. "Now, will you marry me?"

"Yes," she whispered. "I will."

"Then come here," he said, pulling her close. "I'm so 'cited' about this, I'm going to kiss you right in front of all creation."

Just as their lips met, a screen door slammed and a little boy's voice demanded, "Whatcha doing?"

With a great sigh, Jake dropped his hands from around Brooke, and trying not to laugh, she stepped over and sat on the swing.

"Come on over here, son," Jake said. "We all need to have a serious talk."

Before Brooke could warn him, Jake sat beside her on the swing, something popped and creaked, the chain came out of the side where Jake sat, and they both jumped up as one side of the swing hung precariously from the rusty chain.

When Brooke finally stopped laughing, she said accusingly, "You're the one in charge of repairs."

"I guess we'll stand for this," Jake said and tested the banister before leaning back against it. He looked at Brooke. "You want to tell him?"

"You can."

"Your mother and I want to get married."

Ben's mouth fell open. "You mean, we're going to be a family?"

When Jake nodded, Ben shouted, "Cool! But first I want to show you something." He walked out onto the yard, looking up at the sky. "Over here. Over here."

Brooke and Jake walked over and finally saw it. A very faint rainbow of soft pastel colors arced across the late evening sky.

"It didn't even rain," Ben said.

"It's a reminder," Jake said.

It reminded Brooke of a verse of Scripture about God's unfailing love and how Jake had not failed her, even when she didn't trust him. But under the guidance of God's love and with His help, she, Jake, and Ben could be a family.

Just before Ben returned to the back yard and just before Jake led Brooke inside the living room to continue what he'd started before they were interrupted, he looked at the sky again.

"A reminder," he said, "that no matter how much rain there is in a person's life, there's somewhere a rainbow."

A Letter To Our Readers

Dear Reader:

In order that we might better contribute to your reading enjoyment, we would appreciate your taking a few minutes to respond to the following questions. We welcome your comments and read each form and letter we receive. When completed, please return to the following:

Rebecca Germany, Fiction Editor
Heartsong Presents
PO Box 719
Uhrichsville, Ohio 44683

1. Did you enjoy reading *Somewhere a Rainbow?*
    ❑ Very much. I would like to see more books
       by this author!
    ❑ Moderately
       I would have enjoyed it more if _____
    _____
    _____

2. Are you a member of **Heartsong Presents**? Yes ❑ No ❑
    If no, where did you purchase this book? _____
    _____

3. How would you rate, on a scale from 1 (poor) to 5 (superior), the cover design? _____

4. On a scale from 1 (poor) to 10 (superior), please rate the following elements.

    _____ Heroine   _____ Plot

    _____ Hero   _____ Inspirational theme

    _____ Setting   _____ Secondary characters

5. These characters were special because_____

_____

_____

6. How has this book inspired your life?_____

_____

_____

7. What settings would you like to see covered in future
   Heartsong Presents books?_____

_____

_____

8. What are some inspirational themes you would like to see
   treated in future books?_____

_____

_____

9. Would you be interested in reading other **Heartsong
   Presents** titles?   Yes ☐   No ☐

10. Please check your age range:
    ☐ Under 18   ☐ 18-24   ☐ 25-34
    ☐ 35-45   ☐ 46-55   ☐ Over 55

11. How many hours per week do you read?_____

Name _____

Occupation _____

Address _____

City _____ State _____ Zip _____

This heartwarming collection of short stories is perfect

for "want to" readers—those big on reading but short on time. From the story of an engaged couple looking for common ground amongst their dissimilarities to the account of a single mother's thoughts as her daughter desires to meet the father who left them, this collection of inspirational short stories is sometimes light-hearted, sometimes humorous, and often poignant. Focusing on the joys and heartaches of love—romantic love, love for family members, love between friends, even the love of an elderly gentleman for his pets—*Short Stories for Long Rainy Days* will bring gentle smiles, soft chuckles, and even a few tears as readers experience the manifold facets of love. 224 pages, Hardbound, 5 x 7

·····Hearts♥ng·····

Any 12 Heartsong Presents titles for only $26.95 *

CONTEMPORARY ROMANCE IS CHEAPER BY THE DOZEN!

Buy any assortment of twelve *Heartsong Presents* titles and save 25% off of the already discounted price of $2.95 each!

*plus $1.00 shipping and handling per order and sales tax where applicable.

HEARTSONG PRESENTS *TITLES AVAILABLE NOW:*

_HP177 NEPALI NOON, *Susannah Hayden*
_HP178 EAGLES FOR ANNA, *Cathrine Runyon*
_HP181 RETREAT TO LOVE, *Nancy N. Rue*
_HP182 A WING AND A PRAYER, *Tracie J. Peterson*
_HP185 ABIDE WITH ME, *Una McManus*
_HP186 WINGS LIKE EAGLES, *Tracie J. Peterson*
_HP189 A KINDLED SPARK, *Colleen L. Reece*
_HP190 A MATTER OF FAITH, *Nina Coombs Pykare*
_HP193 COMPASSIONATE LOVE, *Ann Bell*
_HP197 EAGLE PILOT, *Jill Stengl*
_HP198 WATERCOLOR CASTLES, *Ranee McCollum*
_HP201 A WHOLE NEW WORLD, *Yvonne Lehman*
_HP202 SEARCH FOR TODAY, *Mary Hawkins*
_HP205 A QUESTION OF BALANCE, *Veda Boyd Jones*
_HP206 POLITICALLY CORRECT, *Kay Cornelius*
_HP209 SOFT BEATS MY HEART, *Aleesha Carter*
_HP210 THE FRUIT OF HER HANDS, *Jane Orcutt*
_HP213 PICTURE OF LOVE, *Tamela Hancock Murray*
_HP214 TOMORROW'S RAINBOW, *VeraLee Wiggins*

_HP217 ODYSSEY OF LOVE, *Melanie Panagiotopoulos*
_HP218 HAWAIIAN HEARTBEAT, *Yvonne Lehman*
_HP221 THIEF OF MY HEART, *Catherine Bach*
_HP222 FINALLY, LOVE, *Jill Stengl*
_HP225 A ROSE IS A ROSE, *Ruth Richert Jones*
_HP226 WINGS OF THE DAWN, *Tracie J. Peterson*
_HP233 FAITH CAME LATE, *Freda Chrisman*
_HP234 GLOWING EMBERS, *Colleen L. Reece*
_HP237 THE NEIGHBOR, *Debra White Smith*
_HP238 ANNIE'S SONG, *Andrea Boeshaar*
_HP241 DESTINY, ARIZONA, *Marty Crisp*
_HP242 FAR ABOVE RUBIES, *Becky Melby and Cathy Wienke*
_HP245 CROSSROADS, *Tracie Peterson and Jennifer Peterson*
_HP246 BRIANNA'S PARDON, *Gloria Clover*
_HP249 MOUNTAINTOP, *Lauralee Bliss*
_HP250 SOMETHING FROM NOTHING, *Nancy Lavo*
_HP253 A MERRY HEART, *Wanda E. Brunstetter*
_HP254 THE REFUGE, *Rae Simons*
_HP257 TENDER REMEMBRANCE, *Una McManus*
_HP258 THE ALASKAN WAY, *Marilou H. Flinkman*
_HP261 RACE OF LOVE, *Melanie Panagiotopoulos*
_HP262 HEAVEN'S CHILD, *Gina Fields*

(If ordering from this page, please remember to include it with the order form.)